HERE ARE ... ABOUT ANGIE FOX

"With its sharp, witty writing and unique characters, Angie Fox's contemporary paranormal debut is fabulously fun."
—*Chicago Tribune*

"This rollicking paranormal comedy will appeal to fans of Dakota Cassidy, Mary Janice Davidson, and Tate Hallaway."
—*Booklist*

"A new talent just hit the urban fantasy genre, and she has a genuine gift for creating dangerously hilarious drama."
—*RT Book Reviews*

"Filled with humor, fans will enjoy Angie Fox's lighthearted frolic."
—*Midwest Book Review*

"This book is a pleasure to read. It is fun, humorous, and reminiscent of Charlaine Harris or Kim Harrison's books."
—*Sacramento Book Review*

This is a work of fiction. Names, characters, organizations, places, events, and incidents are either products of the author's imagination or are used fictitiously.

DEADER HOMES AND GARDENS
Copyright 2016 by Angie Fox

All rights reserved. No part of this book may be reproduced, transmitted, downloaded, decompiled, reverse engineered, or stored in or introduced into any informational storage and retrieval system, in any form or by any means, whether electronic or mechanical, now known or hereinafter invented without the express written permission of the author except for the use of brief quotations in a book review.

This edition published by arrangement with Moose Island Publishing.

First Edition

ISBN-13: 978-1-939661-37-1

Interior Format by

Deader Homes and Gardens

The Southern Ghost Hunter Mysteries
Book 4

NEW YORK TIMES BESTSELLING AUTHOR

ANGIE FOX

ALSO BY ANGIE FOX

The Southern Ghost Hunter series
Southern Spirits
A Ghostly Gift (short story)
The Skeleton in the Closet
Ghost of a Chance (short story)
The Haunted Heist
Deader Homes and Gardens
Sweet Tea and Spirits – coming spring 2017!★

★Want to receive an email on the day this book releases? Sign up for new release alerts at www.angiefox.com

The Accidental Demon Slayer series
The Accidental Demon Slayer
The Dangerous Book for Demon Slayers
A Tale of Two Demon Slayers
The Last of the Demon Slayers
My Big Fat Demon Slayer Wedding
Beverly Hills Demon Slayer
Night of the Living Demon Slayer
I Dream of Demon Slayers - coming summer 2017!★

The Monster MASH series
Immortally Yours
Immortally Embraced
Immortally Ever After

Short Story Collections
A Little Night Magic: A collection of Accidental Demon Slayer and Southern Ghost Hunter short stories
The Real Werewives of Vampire County
So I Married a Demon Slayer

To Mike and Sue Lorenz, who are always up for a ghost story or a friendly chat.

CHAPTER 1

MY SHOULDER BRUSHED THE WELL-BUILT arm of Ellis Wydell, deputy sheriff with the Sugarland Police Department and my new main squeeze. I tilted my head, cautiously optimistic. We stood in the front room of his modest 1940s bungalow, judging the merits of two different curtain panels, one a rich sage color, the other a lovely moss. I'd hung our options on opposite sides of the big picture window so he could easily see the difference. "What do you think?"

Ellis nodded one too many times, until a grin tickled the corners of his lips. "You realize they're both…green curtains."

"Be serious." He was the one who'd asked me to help spruce up the place, and the one who had to live here.

"They cover my windows," he offered, as if that were a major selling point.

Oh my. If he didn't see—much less care—how the sunlight filtered differently through the moss versus the sage…well, then he was a man. And impossible to work with. "If you were my client, I'd fire you," I teased.

"Then you wouldn't have any clients," he shot back, smiling, until he realized what he'd said. "I'm sorry," he added quickly.

"It's fine," I assured him. He hadn't meant any harm, even if the truth did sting a bit.

A few months had passed since my interview in the *Sugarland Gazette,* publicly outing me and my ability to see ghosts. I'd abandoned my struggling graphic design business in favor of making a go of it as a ghost hunter.

So far, I hadn't had a single customer.

It wasn't for lack of exposure. For most of spring, and now into summer, my newfound ability had been the talk of Sugarland, Tennessee, population 17,606. As a result, I'd endured a parade of drop-in visitors curious to see if poor Verity Long was indeed three gallons of crazy in a two-gallon bucket.

At least my neighbors all hailed from the South, where you didn't drop in without a dish in hand. I'd filled my freezer near to bursting and had been fork-deep in everything from Missy Forester's Coca-Cola glazed ham to Kimmy Barker's turnip greens with salt pork.

The homemade bonanza was almost worth the prying questions. But not quite. Truth be told, I'd been hiding out at Ellis's place a lot. Not even fried green tomatoes warm out of the pan were worth one more random knock on the door that led to an uncomfortable half hour of small talk. Especially when it was with someone I hadn't seen since the church potluck in fourth grade, and it ended with a "bless your heart." That was Southern for "yep—you've got problems."

Good thing Ellis liked having me over. I'd brought dinner tonight, courtesy of Lulabelle Mason. The smell of rich gravy wafted from the kitchen.

I had to admit it felt good to be useful. Ellis needed the decorating help. We'd started with the recycling box on permanent display by the front door and the plant stand he'd been using as an end table. Today, we were attacking the bedsheets tacked up over his windows.

I took Ellis's hand, twining my fingers with his. "You've been my rock lately, and I know this isn't your favorite thing." Forget the fact that half the reason he'd asked me to decorate had probably been to keep my mind off my troubles. "But believe it or not, this is important," I said, turning his attention back to the curtains. "Sage or moss? Take a really good look."

"Important..." He shot me a sideways look. "Like for the good of mankind?"

"For you," I assured him. My strong, capable deputy sheriff boyfriend had never taken the time to make his house a true home. He never did anything for himself. I wanted to help him, too. "What makes you feel good?" I pressed.

He winked at me. "You really want to skip to that part?"

"Pick some curtains, and maybe we can," I teased.

"All right. That one," he said, pointing in the direction of the window, his gaze never leaving me.

"You didn't even look at them." But he'd accomplished his mission: he'd made us laugh.

"Anything is better than what my mom tried to do," he said, recovering.

When Ellis had been out helping me on my last ghost hunt, his mother had burst into his place uninvited and redecorated with antique white furniture that he'd been afraid to sit on. The dining room table she'd picked came with a warning not to use plates or glasses on it.

And she'd probably sent him the bill.

"I just want you to be happy," I told him. I'd helped him discover his own personal style and we'd had a lot of fun in the process.

When it came right down to it, Ellis had a great eye. Discovering that pleased him immensely, even if he didn't quite understand how we'd managed to spend more than an hour in a store that sold only lamps.

I'd shown him how to be thrifty as well. We found a pretty white rug on clearance at the Target over in Lawrenceburg, along with a chocolate suede slipcover for a soft, comfortable couch we'd found at a garage sale.

"Let me make one thing clear," Ellis said, wrapping his arms around me tight. "I'm happier than I've been in a long time." The oven timer dinged. "Ignore it," he said, leaning down for a kiss.

I enjoyed one kiss, then another. "Come on," I murmured, "I'm starving." I took his hand and guided him through the short hallway that led to the kitchen. I'd tell him later that this was my last casserole.

Despite my troubles, I was determined to be thankful, not only for the people in my life who cared about me, like Ellis, but also for my special connection to the spirit world. Not everyone could see ghosts. I'd find a way to make use of my gift.

So far, I'd posted flyers. I'd embarrassed myself on local radio morning shows. I'd given a talk at the library. Everyone had been curious about my ability and about the long-dead gangster who supplied the supernatural power to make it happen, but no one had hired me yet.

If something didn't change soon, I might have to give up my new business before it ever got started.

We entered his black and white tiled kitchen and smelled roasted chicken in rosemary gravy with a buttery crust. Ellis gave an appreciative groan. "You might not like all your drop-in visitors, but some of them can sure cook."

I went to fetch a trivet. "I wouldn't need charity casseroles if I could manage to get just one ghost-hunting job." My ever-patient boyfriend had offered to spot me grocery money, but I didn't want that. Besides, I needed to prove to the good people of Sugarland that my ability was real. We lived in an old Southern town—one with a rich, haunted history. But I'd also grown up with these people, and to suddenly tell them all I had gained special ghost goggles? It sounded crazy even to me. I knew what people said when they thought I couldn't hear. "You realize you're dating the town coot."

"Believe me, there are lots of other people in line for that title," Ellis said, handing me a pair of red Fiestaware plates. "You haven't patrolled the neighborhoods like I have."

"Ha," I said, placing the plates on the table. We'd picked them out last week and they were so…him. And they went perfectly in his quaint, 1960s throwback kitchen. Maybe someday I'd buy real dishes again, perhaps some pretty yellow ones.

I'd had to sell most everything I owned last summer after the queen bee of Sugarland, who also happened to be Ellis's mother, tried to bury me both financially and personally. I was digging myself out one shovel full at a time. Although sometimes it felt like I was using a spoon.

Ellis found his oven mitts and drew the earthenware dish from the oven.

Gravy bubbled from heart-shaped cutouts in the perfectly browned crust. ""Mmm...chicken pot pie," I murmured as he placed it on the table. If I was going to be the town crazy, we might as well enjoy the food. "This is Lulabelle Mason's specialty." Her husband owned the Food Mart and she loved to cook, and to gossip—not necessarily in that order. "I'd tell her I could fly if it would keep us in homemade dinners."

"I like that you have a plan." Ellis drew off his oven mitts and headed for the pantry. "I've got the napkins."

"I've got the utensils," I said, moving seamlessly behind him, eager to dig in.

I tried to make light of the gossip, hoping that with time I wouldn't care, but deep down it hurt that my greatest fear had come true. I was the town oddball, the flake, and nobody understood that I was really just a good Southern girl caught up with a 1920s gangster ghost.

It wasn't like I wanted to be this way. It had happened when I'd accidentally tampered with the funeral urn of a cranky prohibition-era whiskey runner named Frankie. His urn looked a lot like a vase, and his ashes like dirt. So I'd dumped him out over my favorite rosebush and rinsed him in good. Not knowing the dirt was...him.

It was an honest mistake.

It hadn't helped that I'd filled his final resting place with water from the hose and inserted a fat red rose.

But that was before I realized my error. Or what rinsing his ashes into the ground would do. My actions trapped Frankie on my property. He couldn't leave unless I brought his urn with me.

So, yes, not only was I the girl who saw ghosts, I also carried a funeral urn around in my purse with me. In my defense, I did keep the lid taped shut.

Anyhow, ever since I'd met Frankie, my life had been one crazy haunted ride. In my short time as a ghost hunter, I'd been buried alive with a poltergeist, almost gunned down in a haunted speakeasy, and cornered by a scalpel-wielding Civil War spirit.

Then there was Frankie himself. I'd left him at home tonight. He'd wanted some alone time. Hopefully, he wasn't up to anything.

I tried to put it out of my mind as I grabbed two glasses while Ellis finished setting the table. "Did you put the sweet tea in the fridge?" I asked, going to get it.

"Wait." He held up a hand. "You need to see this. I taught Lucy a trick while you were at the store with my credit card."

"I wasn't gone *that* long." He'd said he was going to paint the trim while I was away.

"Come on in here, crazy girl," he called to my pet skunk.

Lucy trotted out from her nest of blankets on the living room couch, with half the hair on her face and neck smushed down from a good sleep. She was petite, for a skunk, with silky black fur, a sleek double white stripe, and big button eyes.

She looked up at Ellis with eager affection. "All right," he instructed, "just like we practiced." Lucy pawed the floor excitedly as he pointed to the fridge. "Go fetch a snack."

"This could be dangerous," I mused. Lucy loved to eat.

At the word snack, she swished her tail and let out a happy grunt. She hurried to the refrigerator, her rear end wriggling with every step. Then she reached around and opened the refrigerator door.

"Lucy!" I admonished as she reached in and grasped a baby carrot from a bowl on the bottom shelf, right at skunk level.

"I bought them for her," Ellis said, proud as if she'd placed them there herself. "It's her own fruit and vegetable stash. She likes the carrots and the grapes the best."

This was either brilliant or crazy. "She's never going to want to leave."

"So you see my strategy," he concluded.

The little skunk clung to the carrot with both hands and

crunched heartily, one eye on me, as if I might take away her treat.

"I had no idea she could do tricks." I certainly hadn't given her the chance. Come to think of it, I didn't have any spare carrots to encourage her.

"She's incredibly smart," Ellis said, as if she were his prized pupil. "It didn't take her any time at all."

"That's because you have the goods." Lucy loved new foods, and I'd been giving her a lot of bananas lately.

"The goods?" Ellis remarked as we sat down to dinner. "You've been hanging out with Frankie too long."

"True," I said. Along with helping Ellis, I'd been spending a lot of time with Frankie, trying all kinds of ways to free his spirit. We'd had no luck so far.

The pot pie tasted amazing and I enjoyed every morsel. After tonight, I'd be back to living on ramen noodles and granola bars.

At least Ellis had a way of making me forget my financial drought. He cocked a grin while Lucy helped herself to two more treats, pausing only to let my boyfriend stroke her on the head. She sure had a knack for charming hunky police officers.

Good thing I did, too.

We'd just finished up dinner when Ellis's kitchen phone rang. He answered while I reached down and fed Lucy the last green bean on my plate.

"She's here," Ellis said, his voice guarded.

I glanced up, his change of tone worrying me. "Is it your mother?" I mouthed. To say Virginia Wydell didn't approve of me was like saying the princess had a small hang-up about the pea. It had begun when I'd ended my engagement to Ellis's brother a while back and had gone downhill from there—even before she'd found out I was dating yet another one of her sons.

Ellis and I had kept our budding relationship a secret at first, but we'd been outed after our last adventure. Virginia Wydell had promptly checked herself into the hospital with heart palpitations.

She'd gotten over them, although not the idea of us as an item.

Ellis handed me the phone. "It's Lee Treadwell."

"Interesting," I said, standing. I had no idea what the elderly gentleman could possibly want. Lee was the last of a long, distinguished family line in town. He owned one of the big, old mansions in the historic area and I hadn't seen or spoken to him in a while. We didn't run in the same circles and he certainly wasn't the type to exchange casseroles for a peek at a ghost hunter. "This is Verity Long," I said, bracing my rear against the counter.

Ellis listened to my side of the conversation as he began gathering plates.

"Sorry to disturb you," Lee said, his voice low and rough. He was hard to hear with all the static on the line. "I tried your house first, and when you weren't there, well...word has it you've been spending lots of time with young Mr. Wydell."

Sakes alive. "Word does get around," I agreed. This was Sugarland, after all. "Now that you've found me, what can I do for you?"

He cleared his throat. "I need you to be honest," he said tersely. "Are you serious about that ghost-hunting business?"

"Serious as the grave," I assured him. It might not have been the best choice of words, but I was too focused on the fact that Lee could actually have a job for me. Lee Treadwell was well known in this town, respected. If he hired me, maybe everyone else would start to take me seriously as well.

Lee exhaled sharply. "I need you to come over right away."

"Is it an emergency?" I'd need to prepare. "I've left my ghost at home." Frankie couldn't go anywhere without his urn, which was resting in a barrel full of dirt in my parlor. How it had gotten there was a long story. Suffice it to say, I had no power without him.

"I've stumbled across something peculiar," Lee said, his voice strained. "I need you to see it. Grab your ghost. Pick up a crucifix while you're at it, because I don't think you've ever seen anything like this."

I'd seen plenty. The newspaper hadn't revealed all my secrets.

"Hang tight," I told him. "I'll be over as soon as I can." I hung up.

Ellis stood a few feet away, with Lucy snuggled in his arms, her head buried under one of his biceps. "What's the crisis?"

"I don't know yet." I smiled, despite my trepidation. "But I've got my first ghost-hunting job."

CHAPTER 2

I SWUNG BY MY HOUSE AND grabbed my ghost friend, Frankie—or more accurately—Frankie's urn. We had no time to waste. The sun would be setting soon, and I didn't want to go into the ghostly unknown at night. That was just asking for trouble.

Lee Treadwell's estate stood clear on the other side of town. His family had owned the Rock Fall property for at least a hundred years.

My 1978 Cadillac lurched over a pothole as I turned right onto Main. I swore the avocado green land yacht had rubber bands holding the suspension together. But I'd inherited it free and clear from my grandmother—God rest her soul—and beggars couldn't be choosers.

My ghostly companion's urn rattled on the seat next to me as we hit a rough patch of pavement.

"How are you doing, Frankie?" I asked as we turned left by the Trinity Baptist Church and headed north toward the historic part of downtown Sugarland. "Frankie?" I prodded.

"I'm not talking to you," the ghost's disembodied voice grumbled.

"I realize you'd planned to stay in tonight." Still, his mood surprised me. He usually enjoyed a trip into town. "I'm taking you somewhere fun," I promised, passing the town square. "There will be other ghosts there."

"Yeah, I'm supposed to like someone just because they're dead." He shimmered into view in the passenger seat next to me, wearing a pin-striped suit coat with matching cuffed trousers and a fat tie. Frankie appeared in black and white, his image transparent enough that I could just make out the urn rattling beneath him.

"We have our first ghost-hunting job," I said, willing him to be as excited as I was.

It didn't work. "For your information," he informed me, quite haughtily, "I was in the middle of something big."

"Hardly. I found you on my back porch, smoking a cigar and drinking whiskey from the bottle." I'd scooped up his urn from the parlor and had him in the front seat of my car faster than you could say *Bob's your uncle*. "Come to think of it, how did you get a bottle of whiskey?" Ghosts only owned what they'd had on them when they died. And Frankie certainly hadn't passed away with a flagon of booze—I'd have seen it by now.

I admit I'd given him a few occasions to drink.

He glared at me. "Suds came over. We were plotting ways to get me free."

Ah, Suds—his old partner in crime, whom we'd uncovered on our last adventure. "Tell him I said hi."

He tossed his hands up. "You ran straight through him on the steps."

"Whoops." I shot him an apologetic look. "My mind was somewhere else." Besides, while Frankie appeared to me because he was grounded on my property, the old gangster had to lend me his energy in order for me to interact with anyone else on the other side. It wasn't like I had any special ability of my own. "I'll make it up to Suds. And you," I assured my prickly companion. "In the meantime, we're in business. Let's get excited!"

"Oh, sure." He leaned back in his seat. "It's a real gas." He ran his fingers along the edge of the window as we passed the brick storefronts on Main Street. "Your life plan is to use my power to fix things on the other side."

We paused for a nice older couple to cross the street on their way to The Frothy Coffee. "You say that as if you don't enjoy helping people."

"Sure I do," the ghost mused wistfully. "I enjoy helping them part with their money, their jewelry. The occasional luxury car…"

Poor Frankie couldn't steal anything now that he was dead. He'd pass straight through whatever he tried to sticky-finger, which had to be frustrating. Maybe that was why he was in a funk. Being with Suds again only reminded him how things had changed.

"Look at the bright side," I urged. "This could be the start of a whole new life for us."

He gave me a long look. "You realize one of us is not exactly alive."

"A technicality." We could still be coworkers, of a sort.

I let him mutter to himself while we drove past a pair of snarling lion statues a few blocks north of downtown. The gates were new, at least according to local standards. They'd been erected in 1924 and marked a historic neighborhood that had prevailed in one form or another since the founding of Sugarland. Each lion stood atop a thick limestone base done in art deco style, with pink marble accents and round bronze lights dripping green patina.

Mature trees lined the street, and beyond them stood large homes, most constructed at the turn of the last century. They were solidly built and sat far back from the street, behind stretches of grass and carefully placed landscaping.

"Excuse me for thinking through all your big plans." Frankie turned away from the window and regarded me with a serious expression that meant trouble. "Consider this. What happens when I get free?"

It was quite a hypothetical. We didn't know how long that would take. Nothing we'd tried so far had worked.

Of course, it wouldn't be kind to bring that up. "When you are free," I said, as if it were that simple, "we'll still see each other." I couldn't imagine it otherwise. For better or worse, we made a solid team. "You have to admit we've done a lot of good in the short time we've been acquainted." We'd brought killers to justice, we'd uncovered family heirlooms, and we'd helped ghosts find purpose and joy, even on the other side.

Frankie looked at me like I had two heads.

He sighed and pulled off his Panama hat, revealing the stark, round bullet hole in the center of his forehead. He raked his fingers through his hair. "Listen up, legs. You're a swell dame and we've had some laughs, but I ain't spending my afterlife as some perky blonde's plus one." He returned the hat to his head. "I got Suds now. We're planning a new score. We can't lose. He's the Michelangelo of safecracking. I'm the Raphael Sanzio of stealing."

He was something. I tossed a lock of hair over my shoulder. "Maybe you'll have so much fun with me, you won't be able to resist an adventure every now and then."

"Then I suggest you start investigating more speakeasies and hot dames," he said stiffly. "This place looks dead."

Not dead. Preserved. I loved driving through this little slice of the past. "These might not be the very oldest homes in Sugarland, but they're certainly historic. Think of it." I pointed to a white stone home with a green tiled roof. "The people who built that house walked outside, picked up the newspaper, and read about the sinking of the *Titanic*. They installed the house's first telephone. They bought new inventions like the toaster."

"I'm happy for them and their toast," the gangster muttered. He rubbernecked when we passed a gray stone home with an honest-to-goodness turret. "Now the doll that lived in that pile of bricks when I was alive," he said, jabbing a thumb at the gray house, "she coulda made history with her enormous set of—"

"That's enough," I said quickly. I didn't need to know that much about the neighborhood.

My attention was captured anyway as we approached Rock Fall mansion. The Treadwells had constructed their towering legacy on a limestone cliff overlooking the historic area.

Built to impress in 1886, the Rock Fall estate had been a jewel in the crown of Sugarland, and it still was. Mostly. If you were willing to overlook the green moss clinging to the tan brick exterior and white marble window casings. And if you discounted the way a pair of stately chimneys leaned, as if ready to topple.

The lowering sun on our left cast eerie shadows over the colonial revival mansion. "That's the spot," I said, pointing, and I swore Frankie went even whiter when I revealed our destination.

"Not for me, it ain't," the gangster gritted out. "We don't know what's in there."

"Ghosts," I ventured. The whole town knew it was haunted. "You just don't want to go anywhere tonight." And I didn't even know how to get up to the house, I realized as we drew closer. The rock face was at least six stories tall and appeared to be a sheer drop in all directions. I took a chance and turned onto a small side road at the base of the cliff. It didn't seem to lead up, though.

Frankie shifted in his seat. "A couple of the fellas and me tried to rob Rock Fall in '28." He stared out the window, refusing to look at me. "It didn't go well."

From what I could tell, that described the bulk of his criminal career. "This time, we've been invited. We're here to help."

"Oh, joy," he mused.

"You're right," I said, ignoring his sarcasm. "It is a joy." I was good at ghost hunting. I had a talent for making real, heartfelt connections with spirits on the other side. We found ways to help each other and solve real problems. There was no reason to think I couldn't handle this job as well as the ones before it. And this time, we'd be getting paid.

"See? Here we go," I said as we came upon a narrow driveway off to the left. Iron markers sagged toward a narrow, weed-infested entryway.

Frankie leveled his gaze at me. "You're more bullheaded than any crime boss I ever knew."

"Thank you."

We rumbled up the curved driveway, spitting rocks. I smiled through the whine of my engine as it took on the giant hill. We'd be there soon and everything would work out.

"It's a shame what happened to this place," I said, making conversation, wincing when an overgrown wisteria branch whacked my windshield. The mansion was designed to be one of the grandest homes in the area. It would be still, if it hadn't been taken down by its tragic past. "The man who built this house, Lee's grandfather, was a famous Egyptologist," I said, eyeing an unimpressed Frankie. "Well, I suppose he was more of a hobbyist. It was quite the thing back then. Jack Treadwell made his money selling lumber, and then he tomb hunted for fun."

"So he was a grave robber," Frankie concluded, his expression darkening. "I may be a thief, but I never sank that low, sweetheart."

He didn't get it. My motor protested as we chugged up the hill. "Excavating ancient tombs isn't grave robbing. It's archeology."

The gangster rested an elbow on the car door and eyed me. "Was it a grave?" he drawled.

"Well… yes…" I admitted. That wasn't the point.

"Did they take things from it?" he prodded, as if he could argue it in a court of law.

"That was the goal…" I granted, my fingers tightening on the wheel.

"So it was grave robbing," Frankie concluded, as if he were judge and jury.

"Okay, fine!" My old Cadillac lurched over a particularly deep rut in the road. "It was grave robbing, but can we stay focused for just one minute?"

Frankie huffed out a breath. "I'm not the one talking about stealing from the dead."

"I can see where it could be a sore subject." Honestly, it was good to know the ghost had *some* standards. "The point is Jack Treadwell was happy. He had everything—a loving family, a good career. Crazy nice house." I cringed as we drove over something that ground hard against my undercarriage. "Then in 1910, Jack opened the tomb of a lost king, despite the warnings of a curse. The day after he arrived home with his relics, he dropped dead in his office."

"I heard about it when it happened." Frankie shifted uncomfortably. "A dame I knew used to work there before they dismissed all the servants, which by the way, is ten kinds of strange." He ran a hand over his chin. "She said he went to Egypt looking for valuable, mystical loot. Some kind of jewel."

"That's what you wanted to steal."

He shrugged. "It's not like Jack needed it anymore. Heck, I don't even know if it's in there."

Nobody knew what was in that house. It had been locked for decades.

I tightened my grip on the wheel as we approached the overgrown yard with the dead trees out front. The slate roof appeared to have been red at one time…when one bothered to see past the discoloration and the missing tiles.

Frankie looked at the house like it could reach out and grab him.

"Lee lives in the old gardener's cottage out back," I said, slowing as we passed the mansion.

"Smart man," Frankie mused, seemingly unable to take his eyes off the empty house. "Me and Suds figured the Treadwell place would be an easy score. Then we saw *her* standing in the window, with her face all twisted and melted."

"Who?" I whispered. The windows appeared dark—for now.

"The old governess. She stayed long after the family died out."

"What happened to her face?"

"Beats me. We thought we'd wait until she hit the hay, sneak in real quiet like, but then this little girl ghost stepped out from behind her."

"Yikes." I could see why he and his buddies ran. "That's good for us, though," I said, trying to see the positive. "At least we know there's one ghost in the house."

"I'm betting on more than one," Frankie said. "The Egyptologist wasn't the only unlucky stiff to die in that house. The rest of his family bit it, one by one, in the days after that. The governess was the only person who survived."

"And Lee's father." He had to have made it.

Frankie shook his head. "Jack Junior was off in New York when it happened. He never set foot in the house again."

"All right, then." We stuck to the outer road and passed by the house's long, circular drive. We'd visit my potential client first. "Did you know Lee's dad?"

"Nah," the ghost huffed. "We didn't exactly run in the same crowd."

Good point.

"For all we know, the whole family's nuts," Frankie insisted. "Take the governess. The creepy old bat shut herself up in the house, growing food out back, living like the hermit on the hill. Then in the 1940s, they found her dead in the kitchen. What was left of her. They said she'd been dead at least ten years."

His words scared me. Still, I refused to buy into Frankie's rush to judge. "Do you ever see the governess on the other side?"

"Playing poker and hanging out with the fellas?" he scoffed. "No."

"I guess it would make sense for her to stay in her home." I drove a little faster, despite the ruts in the road. "Perhaps we'll meet her as well."

When I was a kid, my grandmother's sewing circle had often discussed the Treadwell family's downfall while I sat on the floor and cut patterns for doll clothes and played with antique buttons. Lee Treadwell had inherited the estate and returned to town when I was a child. He had taken up residence in the gardener's house and become a respected member of the community. He'd never married. He'd never spoken about his family's personal business.

And tonight, he'd called me.

The skeletal remains of a garden stretched out to our left as we followed the drive along the outskirts of the property toward a cottage on the other side of the hill.

"All I'm saying is if we see the governess, I'm out of there,"

Frankie vowed.

"She might be a perfectly lovely soul. You can't judge her by her appearance."

"If she looks evil and creepy, I can," Frankie shot back.

I kept driving, glad to leave the house behind us.

For now.

I was good at befriending the ghosts I met, finding common ground. The governess might have secrets, as we all did, but if she'd indeed resided in the house alone for all those years after her death, I had to think she'd be glad to see someone.

I slowed the car as we approached the small cottage beyond the dilapidated garden. The home had been constructed with the same tan brick as the mansion, but unlike the main house, a cheerful light glowed in the window.

Lee lived there. As far as anyone knew, he'd never set foot inside the family mansion.

I pulled into the driveway and parked. Sticks and debris littered the walk.

The sheer size of the property, coupled with the sudden silence when I turned off my car, was unsettling to say the least. I kept my hands on the steering wheel, listening to the clicks of my engine settling down.

"Nobody knew what to do with the governess after she died," Frankie said. "Rumor has it, they buried her in the backyard."

"Where?" I asked. I didn't want to accidentally walk over her grave.

"Nobody knows," Frankie said ominously.

Now he was just trying to scare me.

My gangster friend raised a brow. "So are we going to get out of the car?"

"Of course," I said. After all, we were professionals. I even had business cards. I popped open the car door and wondered if the rest of the family remained on the property.

"You should be scared," Frankie said as he materialized outside of the car. "This place is messed up."

Tall oak trees cast long shadows over the driveway.

"Don't worry. I'll be…cautious." Rock Fall mansion was a special case. I knew that.

I grabbed the gangster's urn and slipped it inside my bag.

Frankie stretched his legs. "You ready for this?"

I plastered on a smile. "Let's get 'em."

CHAPTER 3

I KNOCKED ON THE RED-PAINTED DOOR and startled when it flew open and Lee Treadwell stuck his head out. "Come inside. Quickly," he said, ushering me in the door, his gaze trained over my shoulder, out to the driveway beyond.

Lee hadn't changed in the year since he'd retired from delivering mail. He wore his silver hair in a buzz cut and walked with rigid intent. He could have stood to gain twenty or so pounds. His post office uniform had always hung on him and now his blue chambray shirt and plain brown pants did the same.

"I came as soon as I could," I said as he closed the door.

"Thank you for that. Have a seat," he said, pointing me to a cozy plaid couch in the living room. Lee sat across from me in what appeared to be a favorite recliner. A *TV Guide* lay open on the table next to it, along with a pair of reading glasses. He'd circled his shows in blue ink, which I supposed some people did. Beyond the living room, I saw a well-kept kitchen and a set of stairs that most likely led to upstairs bedrooms.

"How's your mother?" he asked, in the standard Sugarland conversation opener. He leaned forward on his elbows. "I used to deliver mail to your house back in the '90s and she always had a tall glass of sweet tea for me if I wanted one."

That sounded like Mom. "She and my stepdad are in love with each other and their RV. This week, she's in New Orleans for the Oyster Festival."

"Good for her," he said, clearly pleased.

"She's living her life as she's always wanted," I said. Even if it meant she'd left her home. I was happy for her, although I didn't always understand her choices.

Parents. What could you do?

Lee ran a hand along the back of his neck. "I'll bet you think it was strange to hear from me," he said. "When I read we had a ghost hunter in town, well, I still didn't think I'd ever ask you over here." He dropped his hand. "Truth is, I should have called you sooner."

Oh my. I leaned forward, matching his stance. "What's the problem?"

He let out a small sigh. "The main house has always been haunted. Don't try to be polite and act surprised, the whole town knows it."

"I wasn't about to," I told him.

He nodded. "Just because I don't share my business all over town doesn't mean I'm not keenly aware. It gets worse every year as we approach the anniversary of JT's death, or Jack, as he was known outside the family. He's the one who brought the curse home."

So Frankie hadn't been exaggerating. "Tell me about it."

He folded his hands in front of him. "I don't really know what goes on in that house. No one does."

"But you've lived here for years." He had to have experienced something.

"Twenty-four years, to be exact." He rubbed the pads of his thumbs together. "I moved to town after my dad died. Dad didn't want anything to do with this place, but I'm the last Treadwell. It's my family legacy," he said with as much weariness as pride. "Honestly, I don't know what to do with that house." His mouth twisted in a rueful smile. "I've taken enough flack for being a mailman with one of the swankiest addresses in town—or at least it had been in the day." He glanced out back, toward the mansion. "I've always seen things in the windows, but now, something else is happening." He stood. "Come on. I'll show you what I mean."

He walked me into the small kitchen and held the back door open. Tiny goose bumps erupted along my arms as the chill of the approaching night settled over me.

"You're not going to believe this," he promised.

"Try me," I said, glad to give him someone he could confide in.

We stepped onto the brick walk out back. Planter boxes lined the way, filled with colorful blooms. I touched my fingertips to a dusting of Goldilocks daisies thrusting out in shoots from a young crop of purple fountain grass.

"What have you seen out here?" I asked, on heightened alert should Jack's ghost appear in the vegetable garden just ahead, or from the small grape arbor to our left.

"This is my space," Lee said, his steps guarded as he led me out into the night. "The family spirits stick to their side."

I could almost hear Frankie rolling his eyes. Most ghosts went wherever they pleased, evidenced by my gangster buddy gliding straight through a row of tomato stakes. I kept close to Lee, on a dirt path between the slim pea sprouts and leafy butter lettuce.

"This is lovely," I told him, careful to avoid the delicate plants. I could tell he'd put a lot of care into his garden.

"I appreciate you saying so," he said, glancing back at me. "Since I've retired, I've been working to reclaim some of the land, as much as I can handle. The disturbances happen just beyond the cultivated parts of the property."

I stared out at the abandoned mansion on the other side of the hilltop.

A high-pitched wail echoed across the expanse, like a wounded animal. It shouldn't have startled me, but it did.

It even gave Frankie pause. He listened carefully as the cry faded. "That's more lonely soul than angry soul," he said, as if trying to reassure himself.

"Lovely." I took a step back when a loud crackling echoed from the mansion.

Frankie glanced at me. "I have no clue what that is." He shoved his hands into his pockets in an attempt to hide his discomfort. Not much rattled the old gangster, and it scared me that this place gave him pause.

Stone popped and timber creaked, as if the house struggled against its foundation. "It's been doing that more and more," Lee muttered.

"We'll figure it out," I said, fighting to keep the fear out of my voice. I mean, at least the ghosts were active and perhaps attempting to communicate. "Maybe they're disturbed by the changes you're starting to make."

"Then it's only going to get worse," Lee said. He ventured forward once more, with me at his side. "I have to fix this place up. I always said I would once I had the time—" his voice caught "—and let's face it, I'm not getting any younger. It's bad enough the line ends with me. If I die with a cursed legacy on my hands, nobody's going to want to remember this estate, much less take care of it."

I disagreed. Someone would probably buy the house, gut it, and turn it into a bed and breakfast. But he was right. His family heritage, as it stood, would be no more.

"You've made a good start," I said, admiring the garden he'd recovered so far. Yet there was so much more to do. I couldn't imagine how he'd handle it all.

Lee paused at the edge of the garden, with the gangster just a few steps ahead of him. "What does your ghost say?"

Frankie turned. "Tell this joker I ain't your anything."

"He's eager to help," I said, ignoring the way Frankie groaned.

We stepped out of the small, cultivated garden and came to a halt in front of a low wall of overgrown rosebushes. Brown, dry branches choked green leafy stems in a twisted struggle of life and death. A thorn caught my pink sundress and I took care in removing it. Due to my recent financial issues, I only owned three sundresses and wasn't about to tear one.

"This way," Lee said, leading us to a break cut into the thicket. I had to turn sideways and suck in my breath to avoid the sharp, scraggly branches.

Frankie didn't bother. He glided straight through a few feet away.

Show-off.

We emerged on the other side and found a formerly glorious ornamental garden decimated by time and neglect. The red brick path bent like a wave had erupted underneath. Grass sprouted between crumbled mortar, and brown bushes with sparse green leaves spilled from their beds, tickling my ankles and making it even harder to walk.

Up ahead, dead fruit trees staggered under the weight of predatory vines, while statues of cherubs frolicked in long-dry fountains, the black paint chipping from their pitted stone bodies.

"I'll bet it was beautiful once," I murmured.

"I'll show you pictures sometime," Lee said, leading me down a particularly dark path covered with an arched trellis that leaned at an alarming angle. The struggling plants blocked the waning sunlight and I reached into my purse for the flashlight I kept on my keychain. My light danced off the clustered vines. I smelled the wetness of yesterday's rain and the stink of rotting vegetation. "Tonight, I heard a woman crying in the garden," Lee said, his voice faint. The dank tunnel seemed to absorb the sound. "When I went to check, there was no one out here. But I did find this," he said as we stepped outside.

The path dead-ended in a small courtyard with a bubbling fountain. A stone nymph stood naked in a large round pool, her generous figure twisted in a coy pose as she held aloft a jug of water.

If not for the shattered path surrounding it, the fountain appeared almost normal. "Pretty," I said. At least it was still functional.

"It's broken," Lee said crisply, "or at least it was." He'd stopped several feet away. "This fountain stood empty for years. I cleaned it out today and filled two trash bags with leaves and gunk. I took out the broken water pump. I came back with the rest of my tools and found it like this."

We watched as water flowed down the statue into the pool below.

Only it didn't flow from her pitcher, as one would expect. Instead, it trickled from her eyes, as if she were weeping.

"Frankie?" I prodded, glad that my voice worked.

The ghost hovered a small distance away. "That ain't natural."

I had to agree.

"Look inside," Lee prodded, not making any move to lead us closer.

I exchanged a glance with Frankie. "All right." This was my job.

Loose bricks shifted under my feet as I advanced on the fountain. With barely a shaking breath, I peered over the edge and into the watery pool.

Lord have mercy. Dozens of doll heads, broken from their bodies, stared up at me through the gently moving water in the basin. Their eyes opened wide, their cracked mouths smiled. My blood went cold. I took a quick step back and ran into Lee.

"Those weren't here yesterday," he said, too stiff to move.

Frankie reached down to touch one and his hand passed straight through. "Looks like it's on the mortal plane."

"Truly?" I asked, wondering how on earth they could have gotten there, not sure if I wanted to touch them. Goose bumps prickled up my arms. "It could be a prank," I said, crossing my arms over my chest, trying to work up a plausible explanation. It was my job to look at this from every angle. "Someone could be trying to scare us." If so, it was working.

The brick pathway shifted as Lee stepped away from the fountain. "There's still no water pump."

"Right." No way this should be running.

"No power, either," Lee added, not helping at all.

"This would be a good time to tune me in," I said to my ghost friend. Frankie had to actively lend me his otherworldly energy in order for me to see any spirits in the area, not that I particularly wanted to meet the kind who left decapitated doll heads.

"I think it's her," Lee said, pointing past another acre of ruined garden, toward the house beyond. A lone figure stood in a second-floor window, watching us.

I shivered as I saw the outline of a young child wearing a gauzy white dress and pigtails. *She was real.* And strong. Frankie hadn't begun to lend me his powers yet and I could still see the spirit, clear as day.

With no warning, she disappeared. One second she was there, the next…poof.

"Who was that?" I gasped.

Lee stood close to me. "I believe its Jack's daughter, Charlotte. The day after Jack was found dead in his office, his only daughter fell from the cliff and died."

"Poor thing," I murmured.

"Told you this place was cursed," Frankie said.

I had to admit that standing here, seeing this place, made me think it could be possible.

"Do you think these are her dolls?" I asked, returning my attention to the pool.

The heads were gone.

I jumped back from the fountain. "How?" This place was messed up.

Frankie hadn't been able to touch the heads. I hadn't tried.

"That's it," Frankie said, zipping toward Lee's house. "I'm done."

"Frankie," I protested.

"Look, babe, I draw the line at creepy dolls," he said, his voice trailing after him. And then he was gone.

I couldn't believe he'd just left me there with a client, and quite possibly a cursed ghost.

I pasted on a smile and forced myself to stick by Lee's side despite the hollow pit in my stomach and the strong urge to beat feet out of there. Yes, this estate had problems, but I'd been in a lot of uncomfortable places, and if I wanted to consider myself any kind of paranormal investigator, I couldn't run at the first sign of supernatural activity.

So I took a deep breath, found my steely Southern-girl backbone, and asked him point blank, "Tell me, what are your goals for this job?"

"Talk with her," he urged. "Work with her. Find out what she wants."

I had to admit, I wasn't eager to go knock on her door.

"She might be trying to make friends," I suggested. I sincerely hoped that was the case. "The doll heads were creepy, the fountain too, but she's not being destructive." Although with the state of the house and the gardens, it could be hard to tell.

Lee stood his ground near the creepy fountain. "I also want you with me when I take a look inside the main house. Nobody's been in there since they found the governess in 1946. My family used to be well off. When the governess was still alive, my father sent for a lot of the valuables from the house. He sold them off to collectors over the years. But I don't know if he liquidated all of it. I keep thinking that there may be something that I can sell or loan or use to make things easier." The sunset glowed red in the west. "I can get my lantern and we can get started right away if you'd like."

No way. I wasn't about to set foot in a pitch-black cursed mansion—not at night if I could help it, and there was no point in going without Frankie. He was the one who gave me the ability to communicate with spirits.

Speaking of which, I needed to find my ghost. No doubt I'd locate him in the front seat of my car, ready to go. "I'd love to help you. We'll start first thing tomorrow." After I convinced Frankie. Besides, there was no sense tempting fate. "I doubt there's electricity in the house, so it will be a lot easier to work during the day."

We didn't want to get into trouble because we didn't see it coming.

"I'll leave it to your expertise," Lee said. I clicked on my light as he led me down the broken path toward the house. "You do a lot of this ghost hunting?"

"You're my first official client," I admitted. He'd learn the truth easy enough if he asked around town.

We walked quickly, glancing over our shoulders. Now that we'd started our retreat, it took all I had not to break into a full run.

Lee stuck by my side, for which I was extremely grateful. "When you come back tomorrow, I'd appreciate it if you'd tell the ghosts I'm trying to help," he suggested.

"I'll do my best," I promised. A chill swept through the tunnel and, as we broke out into the fading sunlight, an uneasy feeling settled over me. I sensed we were being watched.

I ventured a glance back at the darkened house. It stood silent, brooding. I could just make out a flat, iron-gated widow's walk at the very top of the roof.

"This is going to sound crazy," Lee said as we reached the break in the rosebushes, "but the air feels ten degrees cooler whenever I leave the cultivated portion of the property." He waited impatiently for me to pass through first. "It'll help when we get back to my side."

"Ghosts can have a chilling effect," I explained, hoping to reassure him. If anything, he seemed more accepting than I would be about living in a place like this.

I let out a sigh of relief as we stood once again in Lee's beautiful garden. The air felt warmer and the space lighter. Darkness had nearly fallen, and I could see my ghost glowing among the waist-high tomato vines. Thank goodness.

"I'm glad you're taking the job," Lee said, more confident now that we were back in his home territory.

In an instant, Frankie materialized next to me. "I didn't agree to that."

"Frankie—" I'd been hoping to talk to him alone after Lee and I had gone over the specifics.

"I don't have much," Lee said, as if it were more difficult to talk about finances than it was to face what lurked on his estate. "But I can pay you if we find something valuable that I can sell."

"If," Frankie pressed. "If?" The gangster stepped between Lee and me. "We're running a legitimate business here, which is bad enough. At the very least, we expect to be paid in gold."

"Cut it out," I told him. It was *my* business. He hadn't even wanted to be a part of it when we were driving up here.

Lee shifted, as if he felt the chill of the gangster. "Does Frankie have an idea?"

The ghost turned to him. "Oh, I got plenty."

"He's looking for more specifics as far as payment," I said, embarrassed that I had to bring it up this way.

Even through the haze of my ghostly buddy, I could see Lee flush. It had been hard enough for him to admit he didn't have much. I knew how that felt. Frankie shot out a cold spot that chilled me to my core. Lee's breath frosted the air in front of him. "I'll pay you half of whatever I find."

"That might be too much," I cautioned as Frankie stared bug-eyed at me. "We don't know what's in that house."

"Let's both agree to be fair," Lee said. "In the meantime, you're welcome to all the organic fruits and vegetables you can eat."

I stood, surrounded by a bounty of lettuce, radishes and carrots. I shone my light over green onions and cucumber vines. I even spotted a crop of okra.

"Fruits and vegetables would be lovely," I told him. For now, it was all he had. Plus, I hadn't had this much fresh fruit and veggies in my kitchen in ages. It would be amazing to make a salad again, to snack anytime I wanted on fresh fruit. Lucy would be thrilled as well.

"I'll fetch a basket for your down payment," Lee said, eager to please.

Frankie looked ready to eat his hat. "What business do you know that gets paid in vegetables?"

Lee smiled. "Take a look around and pick what you want. I have some blueberries ripening along the side of the house," he said, selecting a basket from a stack on his porch and handing it to me. "There's rhubarb, lettuce, and if you like asparagus, I grow more than you'll ever eat."

"I love asparagus," I said.

Frankie made a choking noise. "You gonna fill up your gas tank with it?"

No, but it was nice to have food I'd earned and an honest-to-goodness conversation with a client who respected me.

"The okra's coming along nice," he said as we passed a row of young plants. "I might have some ready next week."

I walked behind Lee, admiring his hard work. "I haven't had fried okra since my grandmother harvested a bumper crop the summer before she died," I told him. "It would be a taste of home."

He stepped down onto the porch behind the house and waited for me. "Your grandmother was on my route. She used to give me apples from a big tree out back."

"It's still there," I told him. But it didn't give fruit anymore.

"Shoot me again because I am not listening to this," Frankie said, walking through a dented Weber barbeque pit and down the side drive. Lee helped me select a bounty of early summer fruit and vegetables, the likes of which I hadn't seen since my own financial difficulties last year.

Afterward, he walked me to my car and packed the produce onto the floor of the backseat for me. Frankie sat on the passenger side, glaring at us.

"Thanks," I said, when Lee closed my door for me.

"You're thanking him? For what?" Frankie demanded.

I waved as I pulled out and headed down the driveway. "You're acting like you've never gone to a haunted house before." Everywhere Frankie went was haunted, if only by him.

"You don't get it." He shook his head. "I've done death. Curses are something different. They follow you afterward."

Heavens. "Have you ever personally experienced one?"

He stiffened. "No."

"Then you're just going by what you've heard." From what I understood, the rumor mill on Sugarland's spiritual plane was just as lively as it was on this side of the veil.

"I'm not doing it," Frankie stated, his urn shaking as we drove over a crumbling section of pavement. "I refuse to participate in this nonsense. There's nothing you can say. Nothing you can do…"

Then he didn't know me that well. "Southern girls always find a way to get the job done."

CHAPTER 4

WE DROPPED BY ELLIS'S PLACE on the way home. Frankie didn't want to "get friendly with the fuzz," so I left him in the car out front. If he changed his mind and wanted to come in, he was certainly welcome, although I wouldn't stay long. Ellis had patrol duty tonight.

I knocked once on Ellis's front door while letting myself in. "It's just me." It felt good to be back in a place where I was wanted.

"How'd it go?" He sat on the couch, already in uniform, looking every inch the sexy lawman as he went over reports. Lucy lay curled in his lap.

I gave his arm a squeeze and scratched my skunk between the ears. "The Rock Fall property is definitely haunted." Lucy rolled on her back to offer me better access. "A dead girl watched us from the window."

"You officially have a more interesting job than me," he said, his tone joking, but his expression serious. Lucy nearly rolled off his lap and he caught her, standing as he handed her to me. "I get that you're moving up in the world, but please be careful."

Ellis had joined in on some of my stickier adventures. He knew what I was up against.

"I'll do my best," I promised. Lucy snuggled in tight, her soft fur radiating heat. "You're the one patrolling the mean streets," I added, only half joking. Sugarland wasn't as dangerous as the big city, but we'd had our fair share of trouble in the past ten months.

As if responding to my worry, Ellis's police radio went off. *Suspicious activity reported at 127 Main.*

"Isn't that the New For You resale shop?" I asked.

He glanced at me. "You have something to tell me?"

"No. I haven't talked to those ghosts in months." Not since I'd helped a war hero find peace.

He unhooked his radio. "Officer Wydell here. I'll check it out." He grabbed his keys off the coffee table. "Let's hope it's just a few restless spirits. Although I don't know how I'd explain it at the station."

"I know the feeling."

He held the door open for us. "Are you heading back to Rock Fall?"

"Not tonight." I saw his relief as he locked up behind us. "Lee and I are investigating by daylight tomorrow."

"Smart girl," he said, brushing his lips over mine.

"Always trying." Hopefully, it would be less terrifying during the day—although I wouldn't count on it.

I leaned into him and took the opportunity to extend our goodbye for a few rather enjoyable moments. I really didn't want to leave this place, or him.

All too soon, he broke away. "I gotta go."

"Me too," I said.

"Thanks for coming over today." He gave me a wink and headed for his patrol car in the driveway. I couldn't help but smile. I'd had fun too.

I started for the Cadillac and made it halfway across the yard before my poor skunk saw the ghost waiting in the passenger seat. Lucy had never been much for spirits, especially Frankie. She began climbing up my chest to my shoulders, her little nails digging in hard.

"Lucy." I stiffened as she attempted to scale my head. "At some point, you're going to have to get used to him," I gritted out, extricating her grasping claws from my hair. "He's just an obnoxious ghost."

"I heard that," Frankie called from the front seat.

I thought for a moment about separating the two and keeping Lucy in the backseat, but she clung to me like she was drowning and refused to let go. "I've got you," I told her as we slid into the driver's seat.

Frankie crossed his arms over his chest. "Don't blame this on me. That creature is irrational."

"He's right, you know," I said to my skunk, who tried to scramble out the window as I clutched her to my chest. Frankie had been nothing but kind to her.

I exchanged a wave with Ellis as he departed in his police cruiser. That split second's distraction was all it took for Lucy to bury her furry skunk face in my cleavage and jam her cold nose against the soft skin between my breasts.

"Yikes!" I jumped and hit my elbow on the door.

"She could at least buy you dinner first." Frankie guffawed.

I let him have his laugh because just then, Lucy's body relaxed and she let out a heavy sigh.

"Darn it, Lucy," I said. She was dug in to the shoulders. The top of my dress had never been so filled out. But she seemed... content.

I didn't believe skunks were related to ostriches, but if this helped her deal with the ghost, who was I to judge?

At least it would get us home in one piece.

So I nestled her in tight and started the car.

Luckily, we could get anywhere we wanted in Sugarland in less than fifteen minutes. I lived on the south side of town, over the railroad tracks and past the highway, so I pulled out and started one-hand steering that way.

Lucy had begun to snore by the time we drove up the wide front drive, toward the gorgeous antebellum house that had been in my family for generations. Tidy bungalows clustered along the way on what had once been the family peach orchard.

Over the years, my family had sold the estate around the house, piece by piece, so all we had left of the once-sprawling estate were the two acres with the house and a small pond out back. And you know what? It was plenty.

I smiled at my house's generous front porch, with its white columns and pots of geraniums. It was the only place I'd ever lived that felt right.

Even Frankie seemed more at ease as we headed down the side drive to the rear of the house. I didn't have a garage, seeing as the house predated cars, but that was okay. I parked in the same spot I always did, near the long bed of climbing roses that had seen more family cookouts than I wanted to count.

Our extended family didn't do much getting together these days, what with my dad and grandmother gone, and my mom and stepdad going every which place in their RV. My sister, Melody, and I were the only two left in town, but it didn't change the fact that this place held some of my most cherished memories.

Lucy stirred as I parked the car. "Home at last, babe."

"Yeah, I know," Frankie said, stretching.

Oh my. He had gotten comfortable.

Lucy, on the other hand, jumped at the sound of the gangster's voice. Before I could even get the car door all the way open, she'd tumbled out of my cleavage and zipped out into the yard.

"Sit tight for a second," Frankie instructed.

I turned to ask him why when I felt the pricking weight of the ghost's power settle over me. Lucy took advantage of the distraction and I watched helplessly as she made a beeline for her favorite hiding spot under the porch.

It was just what I needed—a dusty skunk in my bed tonight.

"What are you doing?" I asked as his energy seeped into my muscle and bone. The air around me shifted, waking up my senses to what lay on the other side. It wasn't an unfamiliar sensation, but it was certainly unexpected.

"You need this," the gangster instructed, like he was Yoda or something.

I stiffened in my seat. "I can't begin to imagine why." It might have been nice to see the other side back at Rock Fall mansion.

Then I could have tried to speak to any ghosts in the garden. But showing me the ghostly plane right now seemed rather pointless, especially since the power exchange typically drained Frankie to the point where parts of him disappeared, if only temporarily. "What would possess you to put yourself in this situation?"

Frankie faded to nothingness, then reformed next to my driver's side door, as if he couldn't be bothered to go around the front of the car. "I don't want you walking through Suds again." He raised his finger as if I were a disobedient child. "Suds is my guest."

Oh brother. I slipped out of the car. "I do feel bad about that. And I will apologize." But it hardly warranted a power infusion. Then again, it wasn't my energy we were burning. I turned and fetched my produce basket. "After we've made Suds feel welcome, you'll have to take him out onto the back porch if you want to hang out. I need some rest before tomorrow's big job." And I was currently sleeping on an old futon in the parlor.

"Outside?" Frankie balked, as if it were raining frogs.

"It's a perfectly lovely evening," I said, looping the woven handle of Lee's basket around my arm.

Frankie's eyes narrowed. "Fine talk for a girl who can't do tomorrow's job without me."

I'd known this was coming. And I was ready. "That's why I have a deal for you," I said sweetly.

He shot me a curious glance as he glided next to me on my way up to the porch. "I'm listenin'," he said, as if we were discussing bribery or extortion, two of his favorite subjects.

I stopped at the bottom of the steps. "I realize you were offended when I took the job without asking you. I shouldn't have done that."

He frowned, as if he sensed a catch. In this case, he was right.

"But this job does pay, and I do need it. And as far as ghost hunting goes, you have to admit it's been quite rewarding for both of us so far. I managed to keep my house, and you got your best friend back."

He planted his hands on his hips. "So what's the deal?"

"Simple." I notched my chin up. "We're a team. And I'll always ask before taking you on any jobs."

"You'll ask me?" he thundered, his gray face mottling with rage. "That's not a deal, that's a partnership, and one I didn't even agree to!"

Maybe Lucy had the right idea, hiding under the porch.

"All right," I said, starting up the steps. I could sweeten the pot. Frankie always liked getting out of the house. "You help me and I'll take you to the haunted speakeasy to see your friends."

The gangster halted. "The last time, they tried to shoot you."

"True." I hoped they'd calmed down since then.

Frankie scowled. "The time before that, you got attacked by a poltergeist."

I gripped my basket tighter. He did know how to bring on the memories.

"Next time, don't get so close to the skeletons that you knock the heads off," he went on, as if I hadn't gotten the point.

I was trying my best and fast losing patience with him poking holes in my plans. I turned to him at the top of the stairs. "Well, what do you want?"

Talk about a loaded question.

Frankie grinned.

He wasn't the only one. His friend Suds shimmered into view next to my porch swing, wearing a similar dog-eat-dog grin. "Did they teach you that smirk in Mobster 101?" I asked.

"Yeah," Suds said, with clear relish. "It's called a shakedown." Dirt and grime streaked his tan pleated pants and chambray shirt, and a spiderweb dangled from his bowler hat, just as it had when he'd died trying to dig into the vault at the First Sugarland Bank in 1933. "Tell the little lady to break you out of that rosebush."

"It's not so simple," I explained. We'd tried many times to free Frankie from my property and it hadn't worked.

Suds hadn't been there when we'd tried everything from drying and digging to psychic intervention to free Frankie's remains from my garden soil. When that didn't work, we'd gathered up all the ground his ashes could have possibly touched and relocated it to a whiskey barrel in my parlor. Along with the rosebush. And Frankie's gun.

Suds looked at me expectantly and I decided it was time for a very Southern subject change. "I'm sorry I walked through you."

He tipped his hat at me. "I'm sorry I told Frankie to shoot you."

There. We were all better.

"You know what I want?" Frankie asked.

Just by his tone, I knew I wouldn't like it.

He went over to Suds and clapped him on the shoulder, sending up a small ghostly dust cloud. "I want more of this."

I exchanged a glance with Suds, glad that Frankie's best friend had no idea what he was talking about either.

Frankie rolled his eyes. "We found out I need to be reunited with the thing I love most in order to set me free."

Suds appeared distinctly uncomfortable. "Hey, now..."

"Well, I love that gun we found," Frankie said, pacing the porch, passing straight through the clay pots of daisies I'd planted for decoration. "But did that gun get me free? No. It's just sitting there under the rosebush. I love stealing," he began.

"That's true," Suds agreed. "I mean, he actually enjoys it."

"It's the thrill of the take," Frankie agreed, reminiscing. "Like the time we bagged that shipment of cigarettes coming off the train in Memphis."

Suds cocked an elbow through his friend's chest. "He stopped and smoked a few while he was stealing the load."

Frankie guffawed. "Had to make sure they were good!"

"So that's what you want," I said, unsure exactly where he was going with all this.

"I want to feel *alive*," Frankie said, as if it were the only thing that mattered.

I resisted the urge to remind him he was dead.

"I want to lift some ice," he added, with vigor.

"I have ice in the fridge," I offered.

Suds rolled his eyes. "He means stealing diamonds."

Frankie wrapped an arm around Suds's shoulder and gave him a friendly jostle. "I want to get the gang back together."

Suds let out a whoop and I simply stared. "You have the gang. I saw them all at the speakeasy."

"Exactly," Frankie said, as if I'd said something brilliant. "They're spending their entire lives partying—boozing and chasing tail."

"That sounds kinda nice," Suds mused.

But Frankie was all ideas. "We're going to show them the kind of crime you can commit when you truly commit to crime."

Suds lit up. "We can make this our headquarters."

"Oh, no," I warned.

Frankie spun in a small circle. "We can stash whiskey under the porch!"

"Not with Lucy there." I balked.

"Hide cash bags in the oven," Suds chimed, giving Frankie a high five.

"Just so long as you don't light them on fire like you did in '31," he said, giving Suds a punch on the arm.

"I only did it once," he said to me, as if that made any of this all right.

"You don't get it," I told them. "This is my home. It's supposed to be my haven." I'd just saved it from the sale block. It was bad enough I had one gangster here, but I didn't want two, or twenty, or however many dead guys they could convince to join up.

"It's my price," Frankie said, the corner of his lip twisting into a sly grin. "Take it or leave it."

He knew how much I needed him.

"We'll keep it down," Suds promised, like a kid pleading for a favor. Only he stepped sideways and wobbled a pot of daisies that stood dangerously close to the steps. "Damn it!"

"Suds," I chastised.

He threw out his hands. "Hey, I get emotional and I cuss!"

I'd been talking about the daisies. When Suds got worked up, he could move things on our plane. It was a rare quality among ghosts and I wasn't sure I wanted him around practicing it in a gang situation.

He winked at me.

I didn't see where I had much of a choice.

"If I let this happen," I began, "if the place I love, my ancestral home becomes the South Town Gang headquarters..."

"I like the sound of that." Suds nodded to Frankie.

"You'll stay on the back porch," I instructed. "Lucy needs a ghost-free home." And as long as Frankie kept his power to himself while I was inside with her, I'd only see and hear...one obnoxious ghost.

"No way." Frankie shook his head.

"What's the deal?" Suds asked. "It's not like we can feel the weather."

"That's not the point," Frankie said, advancing on me. "She's tried more than once to stash me out on the porch."

He loomed over me, as if he thought that would work.

"Porch," I said simply. "It would make a lovely gang head-quarters." I doubted many gang hideouts had a pair of yellow Adirondack chairs, a swing, and fresh-smelling daisies. "It's yours if you show me the ghosts at Rock Fall."

Frankie hesitated, then let out a low groan. "You should be our torture expert."

"I already have a job," I said, pleased to be able to say that. "We leave at nine o'clock tomorrow."

"You see how she treats me?" he asked Suds.

But the other gangster was too busy measuring out a space on the far end of the porch, by my hummingbird feeder. He paced out his steps carefully. "We could fit two poker tables over here."

"Yeah, but who died with a poker table?" Frankie shot back.

I left them to it and went to fetch Lucy. They could scheme all night if they liked.

The South Town boys might be back in business—two of them at least—but then again, so was I.

CHAPTER 5

I SLEPT WELL THAT NIGHT, EVEN though I suspected Suds never left. But Frankie had taken back his power and I snuggled in with my skunk. We both had what we wanted.

Lucy and I woke early, like we always did since I'd sold the curtains. Morning sunlight streamed through the windows and over the modest futon I shared with my skunk. Lucy snuggled deeper into my grandmother's quilt and was reluctant to get out of bed—until I made her a bowl of blueberries tossed with a Vita-Skunk nutrition mix.

She swished her tail and walked in circles while I set the bowl down.

"This is from Mommy's new job," I told her, watching her flick her ears as she ate. It felt good to serve fresh, healthy food that I'd earned through my wits and my willingness to problem solve…and, of course, through my ghost friend's powers.

I began washing a handful of plump blueberries for myself. "Frankie and I are going to have a busy morning," I said, "but with any luck, we'll get to the bottom of that haunting today."

Lucy snurfled and chewed. I took that as a vote of confidence as I bit into a juicy berry. Heaven.

After we gorged ourselves, I showered upstairs and changed into a cheerful yellow sundress.

It wasn't the ideal outfit to wear when entering a dusty haunted house, not to mention one that hadn't seen a visitor in a half century, but it was either that or the fancier white dress with blue hydrangeas.

If I did get paid in real dollars, my first order of business would be to visit the resale shop and find a good ghost-hunting outfit.

Maybe even an old spelunking hard hat with a light above the brim. I could paint it pink.

I felt quite optimistic and content, until Frankie met me at the bottom of the stairs.

"Time to go," he said, his hat low over his eyes, his expression shifty.

I stood toe-to-toe with the gangster, finding it hard to believe Frankie would be eager to get on the job, especially this one. More likely, he wanted to get me out of the house. My voice went stern. "What did you do?"

He broke into a sly smile that didn't quite reach his eyes. "Nothin'." He hovered, blocking the hallway to the kitchen, and gestured his head toward the front door. "Let's go out this way."

"Let's not," I said, slipping past him, heading straight for the back porch.

"Hey now. Verity—"

I burst open the door, pushed past the screen and stood on my perfectly serene, delightfully Southern back porch. Birds tweeted and chirped to each other. Honeybees buzzed over the lilac bushes that reached almost to the daisy pots by the stairs. The empty porch swing swayed gently in the breeze.

If it was indeed the balmy morning air giving it motion.

I turned to the wide-eyed ghost standing in my kitchen. "What are you up to, Frankie?"

He held out his hands, with an innocence that wasn't fooling anybody. "I have no idea what you could possibly mean," he said, the words ringing hollow. He even had the nerve to look at me straight as he said it. "I am merely keeping up our deal."

Which meant gangsters on my porch and any other loophole he could find. "I'm trusting you, Frankie," I warned.

"That is your choice," he concluded, gliding through the back wall. "Now we'd better get a move on or you're going to be late."

Not for one second did I believe he cared about my schedule. "Now you listen to me—" I began, letting the door bang closed behind me.

The ghost disappeared and then reformed twenty yards away, in the front passenger seat of my car.

So that was the way he was going to play it.

I knew his friends were out here. They had to be. I turned in a circle, keeping a sharp eye out for troublemakers, who were pretty much the only ghosts Frankie knew. "This is *my* house," I declared.

A pot of daisies by the steps wobbled. Maybe I could at least make Suds nervous.

"I'm putting Suds in charge," I added, pointing a finger and hoping it landed on somebody. "He's responsible for any damage," I warned. "So you all behave."

A robin landed on the feeder at the end of the porch, took one look at the space, and then beat wings out of there like the place had caught fire.

Lovely.

I moved both my daisy pots away from the edge of the porch, gave one final mamma bear glare, and left to join Frankie in the car. "I regret this deal already," I said, sliding into the driver's seat.

The gangster merely shrugged. "Wait till you get to the Tread-well house."

We'd agreed to meet Lee at the mansion. Hopefully, his ghosts would be better behaved than mine. As my ancient car climbed the steep rock path, I said a quick prayer for a simple, open-and-closed case and for enough luck to find something of value in the house.

My stomach tingled as we pulled into the circle drive in front of the mansion. Nerves, no doubt.

I'd hoped the house would appear less intimidating in the light of day, but no such luck. Decaying spiderwebs clung to the skeletons of dead bushes crumbling along the gray stone entryway. Lichens ran in tears from the windows. And a most unnatural, eerie silence draped over this part of the property.

No birds chirped. No insects buzzed. I couldn't even detect the hint of a breeze.

I cleared my throat. "We're here," I said cheerfully, to no one in particular.

I'd wanted this. I'd asked for it.

As if responding to my greeting, a filmy figure appeared in a second-floor window. Her white gauzy dress curled around her small frame and a pair of pigtails streamed out behind her featureless face.

Frankie let out a low whistle. "She don't waste any time."

"It could be the ghost from last night," I ventured. She'd appeared in a second-story window last night as well, at about the same place in the house. "Either it's a room across the hall or the same big room." I'd go up there and see for myself.

Lee walked around from the back of the house and waved.

"Lee!" I called. "Come quick. There's a figure in the window." I turned to show him, but she had vanished.

"Tricky bugger," Frankie muttered.

"She was right there," I said to Lee, pointing to where I'd seen her.

He let out a half laugh, more overwhelmed than humored. "All these years, it's been just me." He buried his hands in his pockets. "It feels good to hear someone else say it."

"I understand," I said.

He had no idea how much.

I knew what it felt like to be isolated, to experience great moments of shock or fear, and not be able to talk about them. If I hadn't had Ellis, I didn't know what I would have done.

Lee wore a chambray shirt similar to last night's and tan carpenter pants with mud-stained knees. We stood for a moment together, gathering courage for what we needed to do.

He adjusted the work-worn Sugarland Feed Store ball cap on

his head. "You ready for this?"

"Yes." I turned to the ghost on my other side. "Frankie?" I prodded.

His image flickered. "Remember, you asked for it."

I stilled as the ghost's power flowed over me. The gangster did it with an easy hand this time, which I appreciated. The energy prickled over my skin, like tiny needles. I opened myself to it, letting it settle deep into my joints and bones.

Thanks to Frankie, I would be able to see the property as the ghosts did. I was in their world as much as I was in mine.

Curious, I immediately looked to the window where we'd seen the figure. It remained empty.

With any luck, we'd encounter her inside.

I joined Lee as he headed to the front door. We stepped over the sticks and debris littering the once-grand steps, with Frankie gliding next to me. He passed straight through the dead, gnarled bushes to my left.

Lee paused in front of a pair of imposing doors, his fingers shaking as he drew them through his short-clipped hair. "How do you want to go about it?"

I understood his nervousness better than he realized. "Let's see if we can meet your figure in white first." I could use an ally. "Then we'll see what's in the rest of the house."

He nodded sharply. "I can't believe I'm actually doing this," he said, digging in his pocket for the key while I tried to avoid touching the weeds spilling from a pair of stone planters. He unlocked the door and eyed me before turning the knob.

No one had entered this place since the governess had been found dead. Perhaps we'd see her today, or at least her ghost.

"Let's do it," I said.

"This is the last time..." Frankie muttered behind me.

Only it wasn't. "I gave up my porch and a chunk of my sanity this morning for you. We have a deal."

Lee, to his credit, pretended all this was normal. He opened the door and gestured for me to go first.

I stepped into the foyer and was immediately hit with the

smell of dust and dry rot. An elegantly curved wood bannister greeted me, its spindles laced with cobwebs. The red carpet runner sagged from its tarnished brass stays and had faded to a dull pink. A heavy, banded-iron chandelier loomed overhead.

A dull black stain marred the hardwood.

"What is that?" I asked, my footsteps echoing on the thick-cut planks. I stopped just short of the stain.

"I don't see it," Lee said, from behind me.

I bent down to inspect it further. It appeared human, as if a figure had been burned into the wood floor.

"It's on the ghostly plane," Frankie said, hovering over my left shoulder. That meant Lee couldn't see it if he tried. "Looks like a marker. Somebody wanted to remember their death spot. It's not like it's haunted."

I still didn't want to walk over it.

So I made my way around. Lee followed my steps, which was wise. No sense offending the ghosts here. Although I wouldn't have minded if he'd given up his 'gentleman' bit and stopped letting me go first.

We climbed the stairs, past the medieval-style chandelier dripping with ghostly tendrils of heaven-knew-what. I found it best in these instances to keep climbing.

"It's strange," I said, my gaze traveling to the landscape paintings lining the stairwell, their rich, gold frames heavy with dust. "When I'm tuned to the other side, I see places as the ghosts do." That meant furniture that was no longer there, food that had long-ago rotted, music that no longer played. "But here, in this house, their reality and ours look the same."

"Is that good or bad?" Lee asked.

My breath went shallow as I reached the top of the stairs. "I don't know."

Dirty stained glass cast uneven color over the landing. The art on the window formed a rose. Next to it stood a pair of large windows. This was where we'd seen our ghost last night.

I cleared my throat. "Hello?"

No response.

The floor creaked as Lee drew up behind me. No doubt he recognized where we stood.

The rest of the landing formed a semicircle, with five doors leading off of it: two toward the front of the house, two to the back, and one door open to a narrow staircase leading up.

"The ghost I saw this morning would have been over here," I said, keeping my voice calm and my steps steady as I approached the door to the front right side of the house.

Perhaps it was her room. Might as well go wherever she felt most comfortable, because let's face it, I'd be scared no matter where I was.

The knob felt cold as I turned it. Something on the other side gave resistance as I pushed the door in. I stiffened, ready for the worst.

When I peeked around the door, I saw an antique doll lying on the floor. It wore a black satin dress stained purple with age. Blond hair curled down to its shoulders. Its porcelain mouth twisted into a smirk. I turned and saw the entire back wall lined with shelves upon shelves of smiling dolls.

"I'll wait out here," Lee stated, abandoning my back.

"I'll stick with him," Frankie said, sinking into the floor, not even pretending to follow Lee as the ghost beat a hasty retreat.

"It's just a little girl's room," I said.

A little girl who left decapitated doll heads in fountains, quite possibly the girl who had thrown herself off a cliff.

What had happened in this house?

"May I come inside?" I asked, stepping into the room. Pink silk wallpaper bubbled and hung in dirty shreds from the old plaster walls. A tarnished brass bed stood on the left wall, opposite the windows. I placed the doll on the dusty pillow and arranged her dress just so. "There. Let's give her a nap," I suggested, hoping to draw out the child. "Does your pretty doll have a name?" I prodded, straightening her dirty curls.

And what on earth could possess a young child to kill herself?

Goose bumps pricked up my arms. *Something* had happened to her.

I kept my steps casual, my tone friendly as I strolled toward a bare, dusty dresser between two windows. It struck me as odd. Not the dirt but the general tidiness of this room. Each doll seemed to have a place. The hairbrushes stood in a line on a small dressing table to my left.

Not that I had children, but my friend Lauralee's boys couldn't keep a clean room for as long as it took to dig through a toy box.

I stopped in front of the window in the same place the ghost had stood to greet me when I arrived. "I would very much like to meet you," I said, turning to the empty room.

A weak, tinkling laugh echoed from the landing outside. It sounded like a child.

I hurried to locate the source and found Lee with his back against the wall and his face pale as a sheet.

"Did you hear that?"

"Yes," he hissed.

"Stay here," I ordered. "I'm going to check out the rest of the rooms."

He nodded.

The next doorway led to a young man's room, with a desk instead of dolls. Across the hall, I found a suite of rooms overlooking the gardens. It had to have belonged to the master and mistress of the house. In the front was a small guest room. But no ghost.

"Laughter is good," Lee reasoned, not moving an inch from his spot against the wall. "Maybe she's a happy ghost. Maybe she doesn't mind that we're here."

"Hold onto that thought," I told him as my gaze landed on a ghost with a scarred face glaring down at us from the stairs leading to the third floor.

CHAPTER 6

S HE WORE A BLACK DRESS that covered her arms and her
neck, her black hair slicked into a tight twist at the base of her
skull. The entire left side of her face hung in a corded mass of
scar tissue, obscuring the eye and causing her mouth to sag at an
unnatural angle.

Her skirts rustled and the girl with the pigtails peeked out
from behind her, eyes wide.

I did my best to smile as I approached the stairwell. "You must
be the governess," I said, my voice quivering as I attempted to
sound friendly and relaxed.

Her mouth curled into a snarl and she hissed, a low wet sound
that chilled me to the bone.

"Don't go up," Frankie's voice sounded in my ear.

Wise words, but they wouldn't get us anywhere.

The governess glowered down at me.

"I'm not going to hurt you," I said, watching her grip on the
bannister tighten. If anything, it was the other way around. "My
name is Verity. I live here in Sugarland, too."

The ghost of the governess stared at me, her image growing
stronger and less transparent. The tendons in her neck stood out,
her jaw clenched, and the melted half of her face appeared harsh
against her protruding cheekbones.

Did I dare approach her?

I had to.

My palm slicked against the bannister, and I ignored the pounding in my veins. She might be trying to show me something. And she had the little girl with her.

"I hope you don't mind me dropping by," I said breathlessly, taking the first step, braving the second as well.

Yes, she creeped me out and I didn't enjoy the peculiar way her bloodshot eyes bugged out at me. But she was a person, a sentient being, and she deserved my attention. Besides, I wasn't going to discover anything in this house if I didn't talk to the ghosts who resided here.

I took another step up, then another, trying to pretend that I didn't notice the way the air cooled with every step I climbed. I could be walking into a trap.

"I was hoping we could get to know each other." I tried to smile at the ghost and hoped it didn't come off as a mangled grimace. "I won't take up too much of your time." I kept advancing and stumbling as my sweat-slicked hand skidded off the bannister. I was already halfway up.

"What are you doing?" Frankie's voice sounded in my ear.

The governess stood watching, her mouth twisted into a sneer that showed off a horribly crooked front tooth and several missing along the bottom.

I stumbled again, but didn't dare take my eyes off the ghost. My legs had gone rigid, along with the rest of my body, and I couldn't seem to focus on anything *but* her.

I had to think of something, anything, to put us on better ground. "That little girl is cute as the dickens," I offered. All children were, really. "A friend of mine has four boys."

"Stay away from her!" She rushed me and I screamed.

I lost my footing, my knee coming down hard on the stairs. I fell down several, grasping at the bare wood.

"Frankie!" I hollered, covering my head as a frigid presence swept over me. I tried to disappear into the stairs as I braced for her attack.

I should have listened to him. I shouldn't have come up here.

Most of the ghosts I'd met before today would at least talk

to me, unless they'd let their emotions consume them so much they'd gone poltergeist. That was a truly dangerous state. This ghost was clearly in possession of her mind. I just didn't know what she was thinking, and it looked like she wasn't willing to share.

A child giggled and a door slammed on the floor above me. I risked raising my head. The air above me had stilled. I saw no sign of the ghost or child. It didn't matter. I half-ran, half-stumbled down the rest of the stairs and nearly collided with Frankie on the landing.

"Watch out," I said, sidestepping him at the last second. "The governess might be right behind me."

"She's gone." He glanced toward the door as he dug around in his jacket pocket. "For now." He pulled out a cigarette case. "What part of 'don't go up there' stumped you?"

I collected myself and kept one eye on the stairs I'd just exited while he selected a cigarette and stowed the case back in his pocket. "I was hoping she'd be friendlier." I'd never been a fan of Frankie lighting up around me, but at that moment, if his smokes had been on my plane of existence, I think I would have asked him for one.

My knee throbbed, my back ached, and I'd whacked my funny bone on the stairs.

He rested the cigarette on his bottom lip. "Your trouble is you don't know when to quit," he said, digging for his lighter.

I rubbed my aching elbow and tried to walk off the stiffness in my legs. "I was doing fine." Ghosts liked me. And if I could get them to open up, if we could find common ground, I could help. I just had to be brave enough to try. "Maybe she was scared."

"Yeah, that's your problem," Frankie said, lighting up, "you're too scary."

"You should have tried to talk to her." It couldn't hurt.

"This is your gig, not mine," he huffed.

Didn't I know it.

I glanced over the landing rail. The floor below us appeared deserted. "Where's Lee?"

Frankie smirked. "Your buddy Lee is on the front porch."

I couldn't say that I blamed him. I stretched out my legs. "Dang. What was wrong with that ghost? I didn't do a thing to her and she just flew at me."

The gangster took a deep drag, followed by a long exhale of smoke. He rested an elbow on the railing, the cigarette dangling from his hand. "Are you kidding me? We walked into her place. You tried to go up onto the servants' floor. That's her territory."

"True. We're the first living people in here since the governess's body was removed. She's probably not used to visitors." I dusted myself off. "I saw the little girl at the top of the stairs," I added, ignoring my aching back and legs "Is it safe up there now?"

Frankie lowered his chin. "You still want to explore after what just happened?"

Not especially, but it was my job. "You said yourself that the governess isn't up there any longer. Maybe the little girl is. I heard a giggle up there. It's probably her." I owed it to Lee and to myself to at least check it out.

Frankie blew smoke out his nose, which I took as agreement.

At least he wasn't shouting out warnings anymore as I steadied my nerves and opened the door. The staircase stood empty. "So far, so good."

Frankie gave me a pained look, but he didn't say anything.

We climbed the stairs up to where I'd been when the ghost attacked, then farther, to a narrow landing with a high, circular window. Weak light streamed down over the hard plank floor. There was only one hallway, straight ahead. "This narrows down our search area," I said, looking at the bright side.

A pair of doors on the right stood open.

"The governess was in here when you started up the stairs," Frankie said. "She got agitated real quick."

Interesting. "Do you sense the girl?"

"No," Frankie muttered, "she's not as strong, which makes her harder to spot."

I walked inside and saw an abandoned playroom. Stuffed rabbits and bears with button eyes sat at a wooden table, ready for tea. The ceiling slanted down toward the front of the house, over a child-sized piano painted white with blue trim. A hobbyhorse stood next to it. Wooden block structures had been scattered about the room, creating pyramids of all different sizes.

"Hello?" I called.

The next door opened on a classroom, with three small wooden desks facing a chalkboard and a large hanging map of a world that hadn't existed in a hundred years.

"Ugh," Frankie muttered. "Haunted houses give me the creeps."

"Right," I said, moving on to a set of doors at the end of the hall. One led to a small bathroom, and the other, to a bedroom with three narrow beds. "This is cramped."

"Servants' quarters, what did you expect?" Frankie said, moving on. "All right, you've seen it. Let's go." He glided down the hallway toward the landing. He was actually thinking about leaving.

Not on my watch. "There's still the other side of the hallway."

He snubbed out his cigarette on the floor and it disappeared. "I'm not going into that lady's room."

"We have to." Perhaps her room would help us learn more about her and why she was so upset.

"You saw what she looked like just now," Frankie insisted. "Trust me. She was even creepier when she was alive…staring out the window with that kid."

Poor woman. I knew what it was like to be judged. "There's nothing creepy about looking out a window."

"She went after you," Frankie pointed out. "You should have listened to me."

He would have to bring that up. "It had to be upsetting for her to have live people in the house after so long," I said, trying the door. It was locked. Or just very stiff. I tried again.

I'd seen time and time again how treating people with respect, giving them the freedom to be who and what they were, could make all the difference.

"You don't get it," Frankie said, planting his back on the wall next to me. "You're not invited, not by her. Besides, there's something *off* about her. Don't tell me you didn't notice."

I struggled against the doorknob and felt it give a bit. "If I made it a policy not to speak to someone after an awkward first encounter," I said, pitting all my strength against the knob, "I'd have about half the friends I do now." It never paid to assume the worst. The knob gave and the door clicked open. "There!" I said, breathless and a bit triumphant. "All those years must have stiffened the lock."

"Or you're not welcome," Frankie mused.

I hated to think that.

In all honesty, I could understand the ghosts' trepidation, if Frankie's theory was correct. But at the same time, these spirits lingered here for a reason and it was up to me to make peace.

I entered a simple bedroom done in pale mauve. The heady scent of jasmine hung in the air. This was definitely her space. I entered slowly.

A wooden bed stood against the right wall, covered with a white blanket painstakingly embroidered with gnarled climbing vines. A hope chest hunkered at the end. The roof tilted toward a simple washstand poised between two attic windows, but the striking difference between this room and the rest was glaringly simple. And terrifying.

"It's clean," I whispered. Not a speck of dust coated the stand-up dresser on the wall opposite the bed. When I was tuned in to the other side, I saw things as the dominant ghost did. The rest of the house had begun to deteriorate, but it seemed the governess held sway in this particular room.

A woven bouquet of flowers, startling in its intricacy, lay on the dresser. I touched the silky strands, marveling at the texture and the varying shades of brown and gray.

"That's a human hair wreath," Frankie said. The corner of his mouth quirked when I yanked my hand back. "Very popular in the day. For remembrance, you know."

"To each her own," I said, more squicked out than I wanted

to admit.

"That's not the scary part." He leaned close. "The scary part is where the hair comes from. Do you realize that literally every family member in this house died? It wasn't just Jack the archaeologist and his daughter. His wife died. His digging partner died. They were all dead within a week of each other. All except the governess."

"I got it," I hissed. But I could have done without the artistic reminder.

"Let's get out of here," Frankie said, ducking into the narrow servants' hall.

"Wait up," I said, joining him.

"You see how this place ain't natural?" He gave an involuntary shudder. "None of the servants were allowed back in after the family died. Not that they wanted to go anywhere near this pile of bricks."

"Except for the governess," I said, earning a glare from Frankie. "She was the one exception."

"And that lady had issues," he said.

I was starting to see his point. It didn't feel right up here.

We'd do this together, fast, and then we'd leave. "One more room," I said, moving quickly down the hall, deeper into the servants' quarters. We'd be smart about it. "I think we'll be okay."

"That's probably what the mistress of the house said before she died."

I pressed forward. "What happened to her?"

Frankie shook his head, sticking close—for now. "She died in her bathroom. Horrifically, no doubt." He glanced past me, as if the governess would appear at any minute. "After the family was dead and buried, the governess stayed. She drew a crazy Egyptian symbol on the front door. In blood."

"Why?"

"Because she's nuts," he said under his breath. "They called it the Eye of Horus."

"Maybe it protected her from the curse."

Or maybe she'd killed them all.

The last door opened easily and we stepped into an attic room with a low, sloped ceiling. Antique wooden crates were stacked in narrow rows in a (very) mini version of the warehouse scene in *Indiana Jones*. Stenciled in black, they were marked: TREADWELL EGYPT EXPEDITION 6.22.10.

"Oh, wow. This is it," I said, rushing for the nearest crate.

"Careful," Frankie cautioned as I slid the lid to the side.

I wouldn't touch the treasure. I wouldn't disturb anything. I just wanted to see it.

Only the crate lay empty. "Dang." No packing material or anything. I could see straight to the knotted wood bottom. "No problem," I said, moving to the next crate.

"Yeah, there is," Frankie said, his head buried in a crate in the next row. "There's nothing in this one." He shoved his head into the one stacked on top. "Or this one." He turned to me. "Or the other two I checked."

"Well, keep looking." Maybe they'd stashed the empty ones in the front.

There would be no reason to store all of these shipping boxes from an historic expedition unless they were filled with something valuable...artifacts, treasure, mummies.

I took the single boxes that I could peek into. Frankie handled the stacked boxes and the ones with the lids nailed shut, which was most of them, really. And as I slid the lid back on the very last box hidden in the back corner behind a mess of others, I found...nothing.

Frankie rested his hands on his hips and surveyed the room, as if he could find an answer just by looking.

"This doesn't make sense," I protested. "Where's all the loot?"

"Story of my life, babe," he mused.

I refused to believe this could be it. "Maybe the ghosts can tell us," I said, taking one last walk down a row of boxes.

"Yeah, they've been helpful so far," Frankie mused, leaning up against the doorjamb.

"Maybe if you try a bit of positive thinking, you'd realize we can do this," I said, joining him, hoping I was right.

A faint weeping carried up the stairs from one of the floors below.

"Listen," I said. Someone was definitely crying. She seemed so sad. "Let's check it out."

Frankie rolled his eyes. "Sure. Curses, long-gone loot, and crying chicks. This is my perfect afternoon."

I closed the door on the attic room and stood facing the children's playroom. "So sorry to inconvenience you," I drawled. "But once we figure out what happened here, once we've examined the contents of the house, and we know we've done our job, then we can go home."

Frankie rolled his eyes. "We're never getting out of here."

"Patience," I urged. The weeping downstairs intensified. "What is wrong with this place?" I asked, hurrying for the stairs.

"You want a list?" Frankie asked, gliding next to me. "Let's see: take one cursed house, kill the family, let the schoolteacher go crazy. Add a creepy kid ghost and a do-gooder who works for vegetables. That about cover it, kid?"

"Frankie, you're not helping," I said, speeding up a bit as I passed the place where the governess had appeared.

"I'm just telling the truth," he muttered as we made our way to the second-floor landing.

Yes, well, that wasn't helping, either.

I stopped to listen. "The crying is coming from the first floor." I crossed the landing.

"Hold up," Frankie said, placing a hand in front of me as I started down the steps. "You ever think somebody is trying to lead us into a trap?"

I did now.

"You need to get a grip," I told him. We both did.

I slipped past him, careful not to touch. "This is a house, not a mob shoot-out." I couldn't get worked up about every possible danger or I'd walk straight out that front door and never come back.

Frankie dogged me as I hurried down the stairs. "This is a

messed-up spot and it's not even our problem."

That was where he got it wrong. "This is our job."

I found Lee at the bottom of the staircase, visibly shaking. "I'm sorry I left. I got scared."

"It's okay," I assured him.

That was why he'd hired me. I skirted the imprint of the body in the foyer and fought the urge to beat feet out the door with my client. But at this point, I'd have a tough time getting Frankie to come back. And besides, we hadn't made true contact with any of the spirits yet.

Too bad the crying had stopped. "Shh…" I said to the men, listening for any trace of the ghost we'd heard.

Nothing.

"Okay, let's check out the first floor," I said. When Lee didn't appear too keen on the idea, I tried to reassure him. "You can stay here if you want."

He swallowed hard, his face pale. "No. I'll go."

He looked ready to keel over, but I wasn't going to tell him how much he could handle. "Follow me."

CHAPTER 7

WE PASSED THROUGH A SHORT, wood-paneled seating area and into an ornate music room. I blamed my sore nerves, but I let out a small cry when I saw what waited inside. On a table in the center lay a rotting, half-wrapped human figure.

"It's just a mummy," Frankie said.

The legs had been unwrapped to expose paper-like skin with protruding bones. Three statues stood in silent vigil behind it, their backs rigid, their carved jewels and headdresses chipped and gray.

"Sweet heaven," I said, gathering my wits. "I know it's a mummy. I've seen mummies. I've been to plenty of museums."

"Then you shouldn't be spooked by a mummy," Frankie said.

Lee cleared his throat behind me. "What mummy? I don't see anything."

I turned to him. "Nothing?"

"Pink silk couches and chairs, heavily damaged," he said, eyes wide as he scanned the room, "dents in the carpet where a nice piano used to be. I remember my dad sending for it and selling it. There's a harp, but it's rusted out. So are the bird cages in the corner." He shook his head. "That's it. Nothing of value. Not much light either with the curtains pulled over the windows."

"All right." Then I was definitely bringing some skills to the job. I turned back to the scene in front of us. "When I'm tuned into the other side, I see what the dominant ghost sees. It's not always the same as what's there now." These were objects that had been in this room during the dominant ghost's lifetime. This arrangement was a bit macabre, though. "Why display a mummy like that?"

"Looks like it was for show," Frankie mused.

"In Victorian times, they used to have mummy unwrapping parties." I said, moving closer to the artifacts. "That might be what's going on here."

"I told you this guy had problems," Frankie said.

The statues looked old. As in ancient. "So Jack unearthed a lost tomb." And brought the contents home with him to arrange in creepy ways. "Maybe this setup is an effort to ward off the curse? The early Egyptians were all about ritual. Jack probably would have known that." Too bad I hadn't studied deeply enough to know the details.

Frankie swore under his breath. "Why are we here? Even I don't mess with ancient dark magic."

"If there is such a thing," I countered.

Frankie threw his hands up. "You want to take a chance?"

I didn't want to admit it was a possibility. That would be a bigger problem than I'd realized.

But it could explain why the ghosts had closed themselves off so completely. They were scared.

A stone scarab rested at the foot of the mummy, and I resisted the urge to touch…anything. My trepidation must have showed.

"I think I'll wait outside," Lee said, making a quick exit.

"You still think you're getting paid enough?" Frankie said, watching my employer go.

Lee wasn't the professional. I was. Besides, it wasn't all about moneybags and gold bars, despite my enthusiastic search of the packing crates upstairs.

I ventured farther into the room, past the mummy and the statues. Ghostly tables displayed more fine statues, ancient jewelry, and carvings of small boats. Near the window stood a statue of a cat, its body smooth stone or maybe metal. It might even be gold.

Any one of these items could change Lee's situation, and mine. If they hadn't been taken from here more than a half century ago.

"Maybe one of the ghosts knows what happened to the artifacts," I said. "Whoever the dominant ghost is down here, they certainly saw the relics when they were in this room."

In the meantime, I could try to gather more information among the living as well. If the newspaper articles of the day had reported on the contents of the tomb, I knew someone who could find it. My sister, Melody, worked part-time at the library and was a whiz at research. I'd ask her to look into it.

"Verity," Lee called from outside the music room, thoroughly spooked, from the sound of it, "it's getting weirdly cold out here."

I exchanged a glance with Frankie and we quickly joined Lee in the small wood-paneled reception area. It had gone noticeably chilly.

"This is good," I told my client.

"Hear that?" Frankie asked.

The crying had started again.

"It sounds like a woman," I said, moving toward the source of the noise.

"Same one as before," Frankie added as we passed the foot of the staircase.

"We can't be sure of that," I said, skirting the death mark on the floor. "I mean, people cry differently, but to know one from the next—"

"Trust me, it's her. I can always recognize a woman by her crying. Just a little skill I mastered back in the day. I was never too smooth on the breakup," he said, with no shame at all.

I wasn't going to argue.

Lee followed close behind as we stepped into the parlor to the right of the staircase. It had been a grand salon, designed to entertain and impress.

Lee sighed. "Empty."

Not quite. At least not from my perspective on the ghostly

plane. I saw embroidered couches gathered in the center of the
richly paneled room. Comfortable chairs flanked a marble fireplace crowned with a portrait of a man wearing a handlebar
mustache.

Near an arched doorway, not far from the earthly remains of a
potted palm, a ghostly woman wept.

She wore a black dress and a black lace veil. She didn't seem
threatening like the governess or skittish like the girl. Perhaps
she would be the one to talk to me. I sincerely needed a friend
in this house and it appeared as if she did as well.

I approached her with the same care I would for anyone who
was grieving. "I'm so sorry for your loss," I ventured.

She turned away, as if to conceal her face, and then she disappeared.

"No!" I burst out. I'd lost my chance. She was gone. I turned
to Frankie, who frowned. "What really happened here?" I asked.
"How can I help if nobody will talk to me?"

My outburst had startled Lee. "Are you all right?" he asked.

"Yes." I'd forgotten for a moment that he couldn't see her.
"There was a ghost here. A woman in black, but she's gone
now," I added, trying not to let his relief get to me.

"I'll bet it was Annabelle, Jack's wife," he said solemnly. "She
died a few days after he did."

"I was so close to making a connection." I could feel it in my
bones. She hadn't hidden from me. Or attacked.

No, she just disappeared when you tried to talk to her.

Perhaps if we kept going, we'd find the little girl. Hopefully,
she'd be less guarded, more willing to talk.

We ventured deeper into the house and I noticed Frankie lingering close.

"No offense," he said giving me the side-eye, "but you're
coming off a little desperate."

"That's because I am," I told him plainly. There was no shame
in it.

This house and its inhabitants weren't giving up their secrets
as easily as I'd imagined. And I was even more surprised when

we passed through an arched doorway and into a scene out of an Egyptian palace. It wasn't on the ghostly plane, either, but as real as I was.

Hieroglyphs climbed the gold-painted walls. Plush benches set into the walls hid beneath rotting tentlike curtains of purple and gold. Two tables occupied the center of the space, displaying wooden board games I'd never seen before. They weren't ancient, like the objects we'd found upstairs. But they were strange. One had what appeared to be a checkerboard, only with scattered X and O pieces. If they were trying to play tick-tack-toe, they had way too many board spaces. The other game featured a similar game board, with colored pieces and sticks.

"Is this something spiritual?" Lee asked, taking one of the long sticks and studying it closer.

"I believe these are reproductions of ancient Egyptian board games," I said. "Your grandfather must have been a fan."

"Maybe these are valuable," he said, snapping a picture with his cell phone.

"I also saw dolls and toys upstairs," I told him.

He went pale. "I'm not touching any of the little girl's toys until we've made peace with the ghosts in this house." He reached out toward one of the board games and stopped just short of it. "The more I think about it, I shouldn't take anything."

"You're probably right," I admitted. Carting off the ghosts' possessions certainly wouldn't help us find common ground.

A dark shadow caught my eye. It had jagged edges and slunk like an animal along the back wall. "Stay back," I said, putting myself between it and Lee.

Frankie cursed under his breath as we watched the entity slip into the next room.

I eyed him. "What was that?"

My buddy worked his jaw. "Hell if I know. I ain't your ghost whisperer."

"Throw me a bone, Frank." I didn't expect him to make contact. I'd do that. "Have you seen something like this before?" He'd been dead for more than eight decades. "I'm counting on your expertise here."

The gangster let out a low chuckle. "You think I went ghost hunting for kicks and grins before now? I see what you see." He held up a hand. "Killing people might be in my wheelhouse, but dealing with dead people sure ain't. I used to go to parties, I'd play cards, have a few laughs, you know, like normal people."

Before I'd started dragging him along on adventures.

Yes, but I didn't believe the afterlife was all speakeasies and poker games. "Surely you've met some questionable ghosts." He'd told me to stay away from the dark creatures at the very first haunted house we'd visited, and it had sounded like he spoke from experience.

"I got good instincts," he said, "which means I turn around and leave when I'm not welcome."

Well, we didn't have that luxury now. Still, this was my hunt, not his. "Guard my back while I take a look," I said, moving toward the door where the shadow had disappeared.

The room lay dark. I dug the mini-flashlight out of my bag and clicked it on before entering the wood-paneled study. The air hung heavy with the smell of dust and old books.

I searched the floor for the shadow, and then up the walls to the ceiling. My beam skittered over bookshelves on the right wall and the left. There was no sign of it.

I took another step into the room and let out a small cry as my foot encountered something hard. I jumped back and shone the light on a stone statue of a laughing boy. Or perhaps he was screaming. It was hard to tell.

"Are you hurt?" Lee called.

"No," I said, forcing myself to breathe normally. Just spooked.

I shone my light over a large desk stacked with papers. More bookshelves lined the left wall. When I was satisfied nothing was going to jump out at me, I ventured all the way into the room, dodging stacks of books and papers. When I made it to the musty velvet curtains covering the entire rear wall, I heaved them back, revealing a multipaned bay window.

Sunlight streamed into the room and over the absolute mess

of an office.

Crates full of rolled-up maps lined the walls in front of the bookcases, and stacks of books and papers swamped the large wood desk in the center of the room. Behind it, a standing globe fought for space with a wooden filing cabinet stacked with more papers.

Frankie stood at the door. "Did somebody trash the place?"

"I think this is how Jack kept it," I said, easing past a pile of books stacked as high as my waist. None of the objects had been tossed around, just creatively sorted.

"He organized like I do," Lee said, easing into the room. "I can't find anything in file cabinets."

He reminded me of some of my art teachers. Their desks had been crowded with papers, but also works in progress and objects to display. "Is this Jack?" I asked, removing a photo frame from a small assortment huddled precariously under a leaning stack of books.

Lee looked over my shoulder. The sepia-toned photo showed two men in brown boots, light pants, and white shirts, posing in front of a tomb entrance cut from a rocky hillside. "That's Jack," Lee said, pointing to the older, mustached man on the right. "The other is Robert, his brother-in-law." He appeared quite handsome and sure of himself, judging by the way he posed with his shirt half-buttoned and his foot up on a rock. He grinned at the camera. "Jack used to take him along on adventures. Jack's wife, Annabelle, was Robert's sister."

"Excavation fun for the entire family."

Now I was starting to sound like Frankie.

"Robert died in the house as well," Lee continued. "He saw Annabelle's lifeless body and keeled over."

"From the curse," I finished.

"Probably," Frankie agreed.

I had to stop letting him get into my head. Speculating did us no good. We needed to focus on what we saw and heard here in the house. I scanned the office.

"Strange that there are no artifacts on Jack's desk or on his shelves," I said, "not a desert rock or even a paperweight." Even the statue by the door appeared to be from Jack's time and not another.

"Who knows what's in here," Frankie said, passing straight through the maps to get to the desk.

Jack would have been proud of his finds. He would have displayed them in prominent places. "I don't see anything. Not here or on the ghostly plane."

That meant Jack probably wasn't the dominant ghost in his own office.

"Maybe the stories of his discoveries are exaggerated," Lee said.

Doubtful. "We found an attic full of empty crates," I said, easing past an old-fashioned cocktail cart in order to study the books on the shelves. "And you said yourself that your father didn't want anything to do with the artifacts in the house."

I took a quick look at the texts on the shelf. No surprise they were volumes of Egyptian history and mythology. Then I saw a stack of leather-bound journals. "Check it out," I said, lifting one from the top. I opened it and large, scrawled handwriting stated: JACK TREADWELL, SEPTEMBER 1909.

I showed Lee. "Let's see if we can find one from May 1910, when they would have left Egypt with their find." The crates upstairs arrived in the United States in June. It would have most likely taken them about a month to get back home in those days. "Let's also try to find some journals from the months before, during the excavation."

The September 1909 book was pretty neat in itself. He'd inserted hand-drawn maps of dig sites, from previous trips, most likely. There was a rough illustration of a skinny, smiling boy carrying a water jug. I paged through notes about who had gotten which dig permits for the upcoming winter and spring excavation season and what other archaeologists had discovered.

Lee lifted a huge stack of journals from the shelf for sorting. He smiled at my surprise. "Gardening builds the muscles."

"Hold on a sec," I said, reluctant to lose my place in the book.

I cleared a space on the desk, just wide enough for Lee's stack. "You keep reading," he said. "I'll look for the early 1910 books."

I felt bad. I wasn't here to ogle old excavation journals. But the one I had was gorgeous. The next one as well. Lee and I began looking at them together, with Jack's carefully drawn maps of rivers and cities, with names like El Kharaga and Mothis. And then there were handwritten notes in a large, boxy scrawl that might as well have been hieroglyphs.

"He really loved this," Lee said.

We could tell by the carefully transcribed entries. Still, even though I could browse the journals all day: "I have no idea what we're looking at."

Lee sighed. "Me neither." He ran a finger over a page detailing an ancient stone gateway in a city neither of us could begin to place. "But these books might tell us more about what happened to Jack and his family," he said, closing the book, "or at least more on what Jack was looking for or what he found."

"I might know someone who can help," I said, not sure I should promise. "His name is Dale Grassino and he taught my Egyptian history class at Ole Miss. He retired only a few towns over." I'd house-sat for him the summer before I graduated, when he'd gone out of the country on a dig. We hadn't spoken in a few years. I'd graduated with my art degree and he'd kept on at the university for a while. "I can give him a call."

"That would be wonderful," Lee said, growing hopeful. "And who knows? After you fix things with the ghosts, we might have something priceless here with these books."

Neither of us wanted to admit it, but the artifacts could be long gone. And even if Lee did decide to sell the dolls and games we'd found, I doubted they would be worth enough for him to be able to restore both the house and the grounds.

But these books…it was a possibility. There sure were a lot of them.

"It's a plan," I said, leading him out of the study, back through the Egyptian room and the parlor. Heavens. It must have taken these people all day just to get around their big house. I hesitated.

"I'll bet there's a dining room in the back. And then there's the kitchen, where the governess died. We should probably check that out, too."

Lee appeared stricken at the thought. "I don't think my heart can take much more."

"I looked in the kitchen and the dining room while you two were playing junior librarians in the study," Frankie said. "Nothing happening in either place, by the way."

Even if Frankie found King Tut's tomb, I doubted we'd get Lee back there. At least not this afternoon.

"Did you see anything valuable?" I asked the ghost.

"Nothing," he groused. "The whole dining room is cleaned out. And the kitchen is just the kitchen. I'm so glad I didn't bother breaking into this place."

I relayed his information to Lee and saw his shoulders slump.

"We'll keep looking," I assured him." We continued into the parlor. "I just wish I'd found the little girl."

"It's getting cold again," Lee said, speeding up his pace.

I hurried after him, goose bumps prickling my arms.

"There's nothing to worry about," I assured him, and myself.

Although when Lee opened the door for me, I was mighty relieved to step out onto the porch—until I nearly tripped over a bundle just outside.

It was a doll with a chipped porcelain face.

I froze.

"Hey, that looks just like the doll from upstairs," Frankie said.

That was because it was.

I looked out to the yard and saw the white figure of a little girl standing just beyond the gnarled bushes lining the walk.

All right. I'd asked for this.

Slowly, I reached down, not wanting to touch the doll, but not seeing any other options. I took hold of her around the silken waist.

The little girl smiled.

I offered her the doll. "Is this yours?"

She nodded and vanished.

I held the doll, unsure what it meant, wishing the girl had spoken to me. She was the only one who seemed as if she might be trying to communicate.

"That doll looks like you," Lee said.

"Not really," I said automatically. I couldn't think that. *I wouldn't.* Sure, it had blond hair and a yellow flower stuck in its dress...

That could have been from the yard, blown by the wind. It didn't mean anything that I also wore a yellow flowered dress.

The gangster glided to the far edge of the porch, away from me. "I know you want to talk to her, but this kid is seriously creeping me out."

Leave it to Frankie to state the obvious.

Perhaps I'd try something new. "Can I hold onto this doll?" I asked Lee. Even if I'd rather drop it like it was hot, it was my only connection to the little girl. "She offered it to me." It felt wrong to refuse her gesture, even if I didn't know what it meant. Maybe Frankie and I could figure out a way to use it. Or perhaps Suds would know.

"Hold onto it if you think it will help," Lee said, locking up behind us. He tested the door. "I'll install another bolt this afternoon. Just in case we do have something valuable in there."

"Good. I'll call my professor friend."

Lee thanked me and we said our goodbyes by my car.

Maybe the ghosts would talk to me while the professor inspected the journals. They would have seen me once before and realize I wasn't a threat.

"We'll figure this out," I said to Frankie as we left the old house behind us. "Ghosts love me."

He gave me a long look. "Are you sure?"

CHAPTER 8

ON THE WAY HOME, I kept looking at the bench seat between Frankie and me.

The doll in the purple dress sat, or rather slouched, toward my ghost friend, her head lolling to the side.

Frankie frowned and gave it a sideways look, as if it would haul off and bite him. "That thing wigs me out."

The car moved slowly with the noontime traffic on Main Street. "I keep waiting for her to disappear," I said. Objects that had meant a great deal to a ghost could sometimes take physical form temporarily before melting back into the ghostly plane. That didn't seem to be the case this time. I shot Frankie a grin. "Looks like this doll likes us."

"That's it." Frankie's image faded, and he reappeared in the backseat.

For Pete's sake. "It's just a doll," I said, stopping at a crosswalk for a pair of women.

"You just keep telling yourself that, sweetheart," Frankie groused, arms crossed for the rest of the way home.

He was right, of course.

That doll wasn't just a plaything. She was my connection to the child ghost. And since the doll was sticking around, she was most likely as real as I was. If the little girl ghost could manipulate objects on the mortal plane so easily, she was more powerful than I'd given her credit for.

I'd gotten the distinct impression the girl wanted to tell me something. This could be her way of building a relationship. So whether Frankie liked it or not, I'd make sure she understood she could trust me with the things that were important to her.

Frankie had taken his power back, but the energy we'd used in the house had caused one of his feet to go missing. He didn't even complain about it. He just kept an eye on the doll.

It sagged toward me as we pulled around to the back of my house. "We'll have to find a safe place for you," I said, straightening it.

"Please don't act like it's alive," Frankie muttered.

"I don't get you," I said, shutting off the car and gathering up the doll. "This is your area of expertise. You live in the spirit world. You've been talking to ghosts longer than I've been alive."

He looked ready to spit nails as I headed for the back porch.

"Me? You think I'm the king of the spooks? I'm just a normal, stand-up guy trying to make a living in this place. No longer breathing, but that's the only difference. You're the one who wants to poke your nose into places it don't belong."

"Normal guy?" I asked as he glided through the hydrangea bush at the bottom of the steps, not even bothering to walk around.

But Frankie wasn't listening to me anymore. "Fellas!" he said, looking up at the porch, his dark mood gone as he threw open his arms to welcome no one I'd invited.

Naturally, I didn't see a thing. Frankie shot up the steps like he was head of the greeting committee. "Sticky Pete!" he shouted. "Ronnie Boy!" He lowered his voice. "Louuu." He dragged out the end until it didn't even sound like a name anymore.

He proceeded to pat invisible backs, trade play-punches, and jump wholeheartedly into what was no doubt a gang reunion on my back porch. He even lost his hat in the process.

I climbed the steps slowly. Yes, I'd agreed to his use of this space, but I hadn't predicted this. Without Frankie's power, I couldn't see the rowdy bunch or even know what they had planned for my lovely white-painted outdoor retreat.

But it couldn't be good.

Hmm…I stopped by the porch swing to think, placing the doll so that she perched nicely against the old wood.

That got Frankie's attention. "No, no, no…" He waved a hand as he stalked toward the swing. "That nasty thing"—he pointed to the doll—"does not belong out here." He addressed an unseen entity behind the swing. "You see what I put up with, Knuckles?"

"Who's Knuckles?" I asked, squinting as if that would actually help me see the ghost. It was worth a shot.

Frankie moved between me and the guy I couldn't see anyway. "When you gave me this porch as my personal spot, you said you'd give me privacy."

"I said nothing of the sort." However, if having a baby doll and me out here bothered him that much, we'd go inside. "We'll figure it out after your friends leave." I didn't want to embarrass him in front of the guys and I needed to call my old college professor anyway. "Behave," I warned Frankie, and whoever else was in earshot, before retreating inside.

I could have sworn I heard a cheer go up as I stepped into my modest kitchen.

My refuge was getting smaller and smaller every day.

At least Lucy toddled out to greet me, her tail swishing. I let her weave around my legs while I found spots on her to stroke. She sniffed the doll I'd tucked under one of my arms, but didn't let it bother her.

"You're more mature than Frankie," I told her.

"I heard that," he said, his voice floating from the porch.

Perhaps I should have closed the kitchen windows before I left this morning. But the days had grown pleasantly warm, and the breeze coming through the house felt good.

I straightened, enjoying the fresh air while I headed into the parlor and placed the doll on a mantel with hummingbirds and gardenias carved into the corners. It was one of my favorite spots in the house. She would be safe there.

Next to the fireplace stood the whiskey barrel that contained

Frankie's ashes, along with a fair amount of gardening dirt, and the rosebush that started this whole thing. I reached into my purse for the urn that allowed me to take Frankie with me.

"There," I said, placing it under the rosebush where it belonged.

It was becoming ghost central in here.

Of course, I didn't say that out loud. No sense worrying Lucy.

I slipped her bits of lettuce while I made a fresh, delicious salad. Once I'd enjoyed every last bite, I used the green wall phone in the kitchen to call my old professor.

"Verity Long," he said, his voice booming like it had in class, "it's good to hear from you. You know, I still have that pen and ink drawing you made of Isis. It's right in front of me on my desk."

His black cat, Isis, was my favorite cat ever. I trailed the long phone cord through my hand and smiled. "Does she still let you take her for walks on the leash?" It had been the ultimate compliment when she'd let me escort her around the neighborhood after a summer of house and pet sitting. I'd fed her tuna before— and after. Although I refused to think one had anything to do with the other.

"Isis passed away last summer," he said, quite plainly, although I could tell he missed her.

"I'm so sorry."

"She was old and she had a wonderfully adventurous life."

I supposed that was the way to go. "Listen, Professor—" I began, noticing I'd stretched the phone cord as far as it would go. I was practically in the parlor.

"Dale," he instructed.

No matter how many times he insisted, I still had trouble calling him by his first name, at least when addressing him. Old manners died hard.

"Dale," I said, trying to make it sound effortless. I began walking back toward the kitchen island. "I made a discovery this morning," I said, knowing that would pique his interest. "A friend of mine here in Sugarland may have some ancient Egyptian artifacts in his house."

I could hear his smile through the phone. "Tell your friend not to get his hopes up. Most 'artifacts,' even those handed down, are reproductions. My own grandma had the entire British Museum collection of mini Grecian urns. They were pretty, but..."

He didn't get it. "This man's grandfather was Jack Treadwell, a famous Egyptologist," I added, stretching the truth on the *famous* part. And probably on the *Egyptologist* end as well.

A knock sounded at my back door. Probably Suds. The ghosts could wait. I moved away, toward the parlor.

"I've heard of Jack Treadwell," the professor said. "At least as it pertains to Rock Fall mansion."

"That's the place I'm talking about," I confirmed. "Jack's grandson and I opened up the house for the first time this morning. We found evidence they were unwrapping a mummy." I paused to let that sink in. And I'd tell him about the ghost part later. "We also found stacks of original expedition journals."

"Original?"

"Yes. There are also dozens of wooden crates in the attic, marked for Treadwell's last expedition in 1910. They're empty, but they're real," I added, hoping I was tempting him. "You were the first person I thought to call. I'd really appreciate it if you could visit and tell us what we have."

"Tomorrow," he said over the sound of papers shuffling. "I can move a few things around." Said the man who'd told me not to get too excited. "I can meet you at one o'clock."

"Perfect. You can look at the journals and I'll cook a nice dinner for you at my house after." I'd make veggie soup. Or perhaps my sister had a chicken I could borrow.

"I'm looking forward to seeing you, Verity," he said warmly. "But as I said, don't get your hopes up."

"Wise words," I said.

I hung up the phone and went to see what Frankie and his friends wanted now.

When I opened it, I went stone cold.

A peach pie, still warm, rested on a folded tea towel. It seemed I'd had a living, breathing visitor. A nosy Nellie, no doubt. And whoever it was had left the pie uncovered, which meant she'd known I was home. I glanced to the curtains fluttering against the screens on my open kitchen windows. Had my unexpected guest overheard any of my conversation with the professor? The last thing I needed was news of this getting out. I hadn't succeeded yet—far from it. And if word got out to the town, they'd be expecting results by supper.

Lucy pushed past me to sniff the pie.

"Oh, no, you don't," I said, taking the pie into the kitchen. At least I'd have something to serve after dinner tomorrow.

Lucy rubbed up against my leg. "If news gets out, we're in a mess of trouble," I told her.

But perhaps we could solve it all tomorrow, before word spread too far. Maybe I could get a head start today, find out about some of the ghosts, or at least what might be haunting them. I could see what might have happened to the expedition artifacts.

"I'm heading to the library," I said, spotting my sandals by the front door. "You watch the house."

Lucy's nails clicked on the linoleum floor, following until I closed the door behind me.

Frankie wasn't even on the porch anymore. I didn't see any sign of him or his buddies. It was just as well. I had other ghosts to mind now. If I could discover some tidbit of information, some way to connect with the spirits at Rock Fall or to discover what had happened, maybe this case would be simpler than I'd imagined.

I called ahead and told my sister what I wanted, hoping that by the time I walked into the old limestone and brick building on the town square, she would have already pulled together a reference room full of material. Melody was gifted that way. And I was grateful for it.

Minutes later, I stepped into the main reading room with its lovely arched ceiling and old-book smell. Melody spotted me and came over for a hug. Wisps of blond hair escaped her French braid and brushed my cheek.

"Congratulations," she said, smiling, keeping her voice low as we walked back to the private study rooms off the main reading area. She kept an arm around my shoulder, the petals of her flower pen tickling my arm. "I hear you have a ghost-hunting job."

"It's made the gossip rounds already?" I asked, a bit too loudly. Heads turned from the long wooden circulation desk at the back.

That was lightning fast, even for Sugarland.

"No," Melody said, perky, her smile widening into a wooden one. "Ellis stopped by this morning."

"Oh," I said, relieved.

She tucked her flower pen behind her ear. "He needed to look at some old city plans. Evidently, there's a property dispute between two neighbors on Stonewall Jackson Street. Ellis said he could arrest them, or he could solve it."

"That sounds like Ellis," I said as Melody opened the door to the last reference room and ushered me inside.

"It worries me that you're going into the Treadwell mansion," she said once we were alone.

"Already went," I corrected, watching her face fall. "It was scary," I admitted. We didn't lie to each other. "That's why I need to know what happened there."

She sighed, not even bothering to talk me out of it. I liked that she knew me so well.

Melody had historic pictures and newspaper articles laid out on a heavy wooden table that was probably as old as the library itself. "It's not a nice story," she said, almost to herself. "Jack Treadwell was an amateur Egyptologist," she went on, handing me a picture of a smiling, mustached man that looked a lot like the photo I'd seen in the mansion. "He was by all accounts charismatic, a good leader. Not the best archaeologist." She shrugged. "He'd pay top dollar for permits and then just dig like a kid in the sand." She handed me a folder. "There are all kinds of articles in here that talk about what went on in those days."

"But he was a man of his day," I said, trying to get some clarification. "He didn't know anything about modern excavation techniques."

"Yes," she admitted. It killed her when people did bad research. "His brother-in-law, Robert, did have a degree in archaeology. He's the one who documented the sites, according to the methods of the day."

Then perhaps Robert had written some of the journals we'd found. We'd have to look further and see.

"Anyway—" she sighed "—Jack unearthed an unnamed tomb in the spring of 1910 and that's when the trouble started."

"The cursed tomb of a lost king," I said, supplying my knowledge of town gossip.

Melody smiled. "No evidence of that. It was never revealed whose tomb he found. His party left Egypt in May, made it home in June. They were set to have an unveiling and an announcement, but then Jack died at his desk. His doctor said he had a heart attack." She showed me an article on Jack's passing. It spoke mostly of his business and his accomplishments rather than how he'd met his end.

"The next day, this happened..." Melody led me to a newspaper article on the table. The headline screamed TREADWELL DAUGHTER LEAPS TO DEATH.

"That poor thing," I said, thinking of the little girl I'd seen.

"According to this article, Charlotte was only seven years old. Witnesses at the bottom say she just...ran right off the edge."

It didn't make sense. "Something must have happened."

"It was at that point newspapers started speculating about a curse. Then Jack's wife drowned in her tub." She showed me the article.

"I recognize her. I found her crying in the parlor."

"Her brother—Jack's digging partner—found her lifeless body. Then he dropped dead a few minutes later." She showed me another article.

"What did he see?" I wondered aloud.

"It doesn't say," Melody pointed to a place farther down in the article. "He collected his sister from the tub, carried her downstairs, and then dropped dead in the foyer. The governess witnessed the entire thing. She was the only other person in the house."

"And the only one who lived."

Perhaps it was his figure burned into the floor.

"What about the Eye of Horus symbol in blood on the door?" I asked.

"No evidence of that," she said simply.

"I'll have to ask the ghosts," I said, returning to a photo of a triumphant Jack after his final expedition. I paged to the one under it, dated June 24, 1910, just days before he died. "Look at these crates behind him," I said, bending for a closer look. Their lids lay open and I could see inside—they were full of earthen vessels and other objects packed in straw. His daughter, Charlotte, stood in the background, holding a doll and peering inside a crate filled with more earthen jars. "I saw the same crates hidden away at Rock Fall this morning, but they were empty." It was like I had access to all the answers, but I didn't know the right questions.

"After that day, all the news turned to the deaths," Melody said. "And then the fire."

I turned to her. "I didn't hear about that."

She shook her head, as if trying to shake off the darkness that seemed to surround this family. "It was about a month after. The funerals were over. Jack Junior had returned to New York and the governess had taken up residence in the house. There was a fire in the gardens, in the grape arbor. No one knew how it started. There wasn't any lightning that night or any natural cause. The neighbors and the fire department put it out before too much damage had been done. Nobody saw the governess at the fire, but they know she was there."

"She was badly burned," I said.

"How did you know?"

"I met her."

"Be careful, Verity."

"I will," I said, feeling like I had a direction for the first time. Perhaps I'd make a visit to the gardens and try to locate the burned-out arbor before the professor's visit tomorrow. Maybe then I'd learn what was really going on at the Rock Fall estate.

CHAPTER 9

I T RAINED THAT NIGHT, AND when it came time to leave the next morning, I found Frankie lounging under the apple tree, one of his arms flung over his eyes and one wing-tipped shoe missing.

The birds chirped, the sun shone bright, but I doubted he appreciated any of it.

He didn't even move as I stood over him. "Fun evening?"

The corner of his mouth tugged up in a grin. "They'd have arrested us for sure…if they could have caught us."

"Well, up and at 'em," I said. "We've got a job to do."

He lifted his arm and cracked open an eye.

I probably shouldn't have picked that moment to take the doll from under my arm and jiggle it at him.

The gangster slammed his eyes shut. "You got a funny way of asking for help."

"I'm sorry." He made it too easy to mess with him. "But you still have to get up. A deal's a deal. You filled my porch with spooks. Now you're going to show me the other side."

He uncoiled from the ground like a dangerous snake and I could see why he'd inspired fear when he was alive.

"I've got a better idea," he said, eyeing me like the ruthless gangster he was. "The guys and I discussed a few things last night." He looked me up and down like I was a commodity. "And if we're gonna get anything done these days, we need a person on the outside."

"A what?" I asked.

"A runner." He grinned. "A live body."

He couldn't be serious. "I'm not joining your gang," I stated. "No way. No how."

"There are perks," he said, casually removing his hat and brushing the dust off.

"Like a bullet hole to the forehead? No, thanks." I didn't even want to see what had gone down in my backyard now that the gangsters had free rein.

"It's definitely better than ghost hunting," he assured me.

"Are you done?"

He shrugged. "We'll talk about it later." He returned his hat to his head. "In the meantime, I've got plenty to do here that doesn't involve putting my neck on the line so you can get paid in salad fixings."

"If you go back on your promise," I warned sharply, "I'll go back on mine."

His eyes widened before he broke into a sly grin. "See? That kind of attitude is why you'd be a valuable member of our organization."

"Frankie," I ground out.

"We'll talk about it in the car," he stated, his helpfulness making me instantly suspicious.

I held his gaze, as if I could guess his angle by staring at him, and sort of through him.

He merely raised his brows.

"All right," I said, letting him walk me to my ancient green Cadillac. We'd play his game. I was getting what I wanted. For now.

The car smelled musty from last night's drizzle. I couldn't remember a time when the land yacht had been one hundred percent waterproof.

I placed my bag on the passenger-side floor and the doll in the backseat, where Frankie didn't have to look at her. He disappeared and then reappeared in the passenger seat.

He was making this too easy. Something was up.

I slid into the car and we pulled out slowly, the rock driveway crackling under the tires as we eased along the side of the house.

"Stop," Frankie ordered when we'd reached the front.

I knew there'd be a catch. "What?" I asked, putting the car in park.

He raised a hand. "I need to give you something. The next second, his power slammed into me in a wave of sharp energy that shook me to my core.

"Turn it down," I ordered, whooshing out a breath. I clung to the steering wheel, trying to center myself as the hot energy sank into my bones, warming me from the inside out.

"Whoops." He adjusted his power, but he didn't apologize. The energy transfer eased a little, but I still felt every hair on my arms stand at attention. "There," he said. "You're all set. You can see the other side."

True. However, I couldn't help but notice that the gangster had arranged it so I could not see what was going on in my own backyard.

I shook out my arms, trying to get rid of the prickling sensation of the power transfer. Shouts and laughter echoed from my backyard. "It sounds like a party back there," I said, cranking down the window. Yep, definitely out of hand.

"More of a get-together," the gangster shot back.

I leaned an elbow on the window edge. "Be honest with me, Frankie. How many people did you invite?"

He made a show of looking at his wristwatch. "You're going to be late. You should go." He disappeared and then reappeared standing outside the passenger-side window. He leaned on the window, his head poking through the glass. "I'll stay and guard the fort."

Hardly. "I need you."

He glanced toward the backyard. "I haven't hung with Suds and the guys enough since you trapped me."

Guilt trip time. "You saw them at the speakeasy. They tried to shoot me."

He waved me off. "They're over that. Well, all except for Crazy Louie. He still wants to plug you, but he's visiting his sister. She haunts a convent in Omaha."

"Great." This was my life now.

He gave an almost guilty shrug. "Let the boys have a little fun. You do want somebody keeping an eye on the place, right?"

Dang him. I didn't appreciate him bailing on my first real ghost hunt.

Despite what he said, Frankie had a pretty good handle on the other side. He was a natural at reading situations and knowing how to fit in. "You planned this." He'd lured me out of the backyard, turned on my power, and now he was going to make me do this alone. "You purposely tricked me."

Frankie held out his hands in a gesture of surrender. "It's what I do."

Much to my regret.

But he had kept his promise—he'd given me his power. Heaven knew what would happen to my house when I was gone, even with Frankie there, much less with him absent.

"Fine." I *ka-chunked* the car into gear. "I'll handle it by myself." I couldn't force him to do the right thing. "I have your urn. You can join me if you feel guilty later."

"Not likely," he said, gliding toward the backyard.

"You're the most unreliable criminal I know!" I yelled out the window at him.

He merely waved.

"Jerk face," I muttered under my breath.

If he heard, he didn't care.

No, he'd just spend the day with his friends, kicking up his heels in the place I loved and cherished, while I faced…whatever lurked inside Rock Fall mansion.

I tugged my hair into a ponytail and secured it with one of the bands I kept in the otherwise empty ashtray of the car.

Frankie was not going to get away with this. If I could complete this job at the mansion, if we made any money, the first thing I was going to do was build Frankie a shed out by the pond—his gang could meet out there and not anywhere near my private home.

I cringed as a jazz band started up, playing a ghostly rendition of the "East St. Louis Toodle-Oo." A girl my age shouldn't even know what that sounded like, and I wouldn't have if Frankie didn't hum it all the time.

I cranked up my window and refused to give him another thought as I headed north, toward the swanky part of town.

It'll get better, I told myself.

It had to.

One thing was certain, I never thought I'd be heading to a haunted house in order to get some peace and quiet.

I pulled up to the Treadwell mansion five minutes early, which would have filled me with pride if I hadn't found Ovis Dupree, investigative reporter for the *Shady Acres Senior Living Center Gazette*, standing on the porch, grilling my old professor. Ovis was eighty if he was a day. And he didn't know the meaning of retirement.

Rats! This was worse than losing Frankie. I parked the car and grabbed my bag. I'd get the doll later.

Dale Grassino stood with his back to me, in his usual uniform of khaki pants and white button-down. I'd have recognized him from his tan, bald head and wiry frame alone.

Ovis stood way too close, notebook in hand, hanging on every word my professor had better not be saying.

I'd bet my bottom dollar Ovis had been tipped off by whoever left that pie.

I took the steps two at a time. "Professor Grassino," I said, giving my professor a hug while at the same time inserting myself between him and the reporter. Hopefully, he hadn't said much. The professor always thought before he spoke, which was a quality I admired at that moment. I hadn't told him the journals, as well as the search for the artifacts, were secret.

Unfortunately, Ovis was smart and not the type who believed

in keeping anything private. I turned to the short, mahogany-skinned reporter, whose white sneakers peeked out from under his black dress pants. "Ovis," I said, acknowledging him. He had sharp eyes and a kind grin. "See, Professor? I told you Verity and I were old friends." He winked at me. "How's your mother?"

"Don't you start," I told him. He didn't care about my mother unless she was making news in Sugarland. I turned to Professor Grassino. "I'm sorry if there was any confusion here. I appreciate you coming down."

Ovis took a picture.

"There's nothing newsworthy about this. I'm just standing here with an old friend," I told him.

"About to enter a house that has been locked down for the last seventy years." Ovis rested the camera on his chin, as if I should fill in the rest.

The reporter might be bluffing. He might not know a thing. *Or he might know way too much.*

Either way, the last thing we needed was publicity, not with possible antiquities in the house and a ghostly investigation barely underway.

"I already gave you a plum story," I told him. The exclusive about how Ellis and I had solved the murder of the town banker had gotten the octogenarian bumped up to official guest reporter for the *Sugarland Gazette.*

He tilted his head. "And yet Professor Grassino here tells me that you've called him in on your first ghost-hunting investigation."

"That's ridiculous," Professor Grassino said. "There's no such thing as ghosts."

"You can't bait us. It won't work," I said to Ovis, even as I felt myself begin to sweat.

Just then, Lee walked up from the back garden.

Ovis turned to him. "Lee!" he said warmly. "I miss seeing you since you retired. And my wife doesn't bake those shortbread cookies anymore. I knew she was making them for you." He waited near the steps as Lee trudged up. "Let me be one of the first people inside the house."

Lee knew Ovis's game, but shook his hand anyway. "Tell Vera she's welcome to drop by with cookies. As for the house," he said, pulling the keys out and moving toward the door, "we've already been in."

"Then you won't mind me taking a look," Ovis concluded. "I can do a fantastic write-up on your family history. It'll be in both papers."

Lee inserted the key in the lock and glanced at me. "This lock is ice cold."

Ovis took his picture.

"You don't give up, do you?" I asked the reporter.

The air on the porch had grown a bit chilly. Maybe it was the breeze.

Ovis grinned. "It's my curse. I've got to know."

Both Lee and I stared at him when he said *curse.*

Ovis dropped the smile and shrugged. "Ghost investigation. Egyptian artifacts. It's a good story."

Just then, a shot of wind whipped around the house. Professor Grassino braced himself. I leaned against the house. Ovis stumbled backward and fell off the porch.

"Ovis!" I called, rushing down the steps to where he lay on his back in the grass. He might be too persistent for his own good, but his wife had been nothing but sweet to my grandmother back in the day and I absolutely could not tell her that her husband had gotten hurt on my watch.

The old reporter lay with his camera on his chest, chuckling up at the sky. "It pushed me!"

"It was the wind," I said, helping him as he tried to sit. I was tuned in and I hadn't seen anything, although I hadn't been looking. And ghosts could be quick when they wanted to get the jump on someone—living or dead. "I'll call Vera." She could pick him up.

"You'll do no such thing," he said, almost fighting me as I helped him to his feet. He reached down for his ball cap. "Did you see me go flying off there? I wish I had a picture of that."

He was lucky he didn't break a hip.

"We're going in without you," I told him as I watched Lee usher Professor Grassino inside. "I hope you can understand."

"I'll wait," Ovis said, as if that were the third option.

I sighed and he smiled.

"Behave," I said, heading for the house.

We'd just have to conclude our business quickly, then—before Ovis spilled the beans and we had the whole town watching.

I slipped inside and twisted the door bolt behind me, locking us inside a haunted, possibly cursed house.

Perhaps this had not been the best career choice.

Professor Grassino shook his head. "People amaze me. We might have some wonderful, historical journals in this house and all that reporter wants to talk about is ghosts."

"I know you're not a believer." He was one of those 'just the facts' types, which I suppose had worked out well for him.

Perhaps the ghosts and I could enlighten him. I didn't want to shock my old teacher, but I didn't think he'd believe me if I told him what had brought me here.

He glanced around the impressive foyer. "Now what do you want to show me?"

"A ghost," I gasped as a figure of a man shimmered into view at the bottom of the staircase, lying prone—right on top of the death marker. I took a quick step back, surprised at the suddenness of it all.

"Be serious," the professor remarked. Even as he spoke, he glanced around him. "I think I'm standing under a vent."

"The chill would be *him*," I murmured. The figure grew more distinct, fitting exactly over the mark on the floor, his face down, his arms sprawled out in front and his legs tangled behind.

I could see now that he wore a white shirt with sleeves rolled to the elbows. He stirred, pushing up from the floor, and I recognized Robert, Jack's exploring partner.

He stood shakily, brushing away dust I couldn't see, his shirt gaping half open, his hair mussed. Despite his state, he cut a handsome figure as he tried to right himself. "I'm sorry you have to see me this way," he said, out of breath. He gestured toward his death spot. "This is the fastest way for me to..." He seemed at a loss for words.

"Show yourself?" I supplied.

"Yes," he said plainly. "This is an oddly comforting place."

Poor thing. "I've never seen a death spot used that way." Not that I'd had much experience.

Professor Grassino stared at me. "What are you doing?" he asked, in the same tone he used when someone acted up in class.

"Give me a second," I told him. He wouldn't believe me anyway.

I let out a sigh and focused on Robert. It felt so good to actually speak to one of the ghosts in the house and have the ghost respond.

"If it's not too painful," I said to the ghost, "can you tell me how you died?"

Robert appeared distinctly uncomfortable and remained rooted to the spot. "The curse."

"But how?" I pressed. I didn't understand how some unseen force could just kill a person.

Robert kept an eye out, as if it could still get him. "I don't know how." He let out a short laugh that reminded me more of the charmer I suspected he'd been. "When I saw you yesterday, I knew I had to warn you." He began to take a step toward me before holding back. "We brought something...terrible back," he added, his voice heavy with regret. "You need to get out now. Take those two as well," he said, glancing to my companions.

I turned and saw Lee wide-eyed, frozen in place to my left, and the professor on my right, looking at me like I'd disappointed him greatly.

"There's no time to debate," Robert insisted. "I can't take form again. I don't want to anger it. But I'm not going to stand by and watch you get hurt. You saw the presence in the study," Robert warned. "You can still leave."

"There really is a ghost," I said to my old teacher. "He's right here. He says there is a cursed entity and we need to get out of the house." I wasn't quite sure I wanted to follow Robert's advice. It would mean the end of our ghost hunt. But he deserved to be heard.

The professor huffed in annoyance. "I'm not here for super-natural hocus-pocus. I drove all this way to see the journals. Frankly, Verity, I expected better from you."

Robert tilted his chin up. "Normally, I'd be honored to show my work, but I can't let you in there."

"Where's the study?" the professor asked Lee.

My client pointed toward the parlor. "Back two rooms, in the rear of the house."

"Thank you." He turned to me. "Now stop wasting time and come along."

The ghost broke away from his death mark and, shaking, stood in front of the professor, blocking his path to the study. "No, sir. I can't allow it. I won't allow it."

"Don't move," I told the professor. It wouldn't hurt him to walk through Robert, but it might upset the ghost even more. Besides, Robert might have a point. There had been a dark presence in the study last time. If it was there now, we should avoid it. We could always come back.

The ghost grew frantic. "It grows stronger with every death. You're putting us all at great risk!"

Professor Grassino walked straight through Robert. "This is ridiculous," he said. "Do you want my help or not?"

"Foolish!" Robert roared. "Ungrateful! Inconsiderate!" he raged.

Smoke rose from his death spot.

"You see that?" Lee gasped.

Yes. And from the look on the professor's face, he could as well.

"You think you can win, but you can't!" Robert raged. "None of us can!" The marked floor curled and blackened as if singed by a branding iron.

Robert began to fade, his energy rapidly depleting. "Listen to me. It *will* come for you. I can't stop it..." he said, his ghost fading into the place where he died until he disappeared completely.

"So that was Robert," I said to my two shaken companions.

"That was real," the professor said, as if he couldn't quite believe what he was seeing clear as day on the mortal plane—the smoking outline of a body branded into the floor.

"I have a fire extinguisher in my car," Lee said, "just in case." He stepped back. "I'll go get it." He appeared a bit relieved to be heading for the door.

The professor remained where he was. His hand shook as he wiped the sweat from his forehead, despite the chill that lingered in the air. "I'm sorry I didn't take your word for it," he said. "I needed proof to ever believe and, well, there we have it."

"I'm trying to make it as a ghost hunter," I told him. "This is my first case, so any help you can give, I'd really appreciate."

He clapped me on the shoulder and gave it a squeeze. "I'll do my best," he said, still a bit rattled. "I'm proud of you, Verity. I always knew you'd follow your own path."

"Thanks." I grinned, warming to his praise.

Lee returned, hauling a fire extinguisher. I saw no more sign of Robert, which saddened me. I would have liked to ask him more about the house and what he and Jack had found in Egypt. And I would have liked the chance to thank him for his warning. He'd meant well.

Perhaps he'd return, because we did need to show the professor those journals.

But first... "Now that you believe me about spirits, I'd like to get your take on some ghostly artifacts." Then, if he ran across something related to them in the journals, we'd know.

"Ghostly artifacts," the professor repeated, following me toward the music room. "I can hardly imagine." He stuck close as we passed through the paneled reception room, his arms folded firmly over his chest. "Will I be able to see them?"

"You probably won't," I said, "but I can describe them to you."

We entered the pink-carpeted music room. The mummy lay on the slab, surrounded by its stone attendants, and I was able to notice more of it now, without the shock of first discovery. The bones of one foot thrust from blackened wrappings, as did a leg bone. Its arms crossed over its chest, as if in silent prayer, and gold coins covered dead eyes.

"There used to be a mummy here," I said to the professor. "It's very clear on the ghostly plane. I believe they attempted to unwrap it. There were three female statues surrounding it—"

He stared at the ruined furniture, the lamps, and the rusted harp as if they were going to haul off and bite him. "I wish I could see what you do." He dug in his satchel and withdrew a notebook. "Do me a favor. Draw these ghostly artifacts."

He handed me the notebook and a pen, and I took them as if I'd just received a class assignment. "All right." I'd always been good at sketching, especially when an object was right in front of me.

I took one last glance at the professor, who looked as if he were the one seeing ghosts. Then I got to work. I drew the mummy with its undressed leg, as well as the statues, making sure to detail how each wore braided hair in a distinct, elaborate style. Jewels covered each woman's chest, stopping just above her small bare breasts.

My professor took in every detail as the images took shape under my quickly moving pencil. "As I live and breathe," he murmured. "You really do have a gift. Take a look at the statues' legs. If there are any inscriptions left, they should tell us more."

I crouched in front of the far left statue. The paint had worn off, but I could see time-roughened cuts in the stone, forming shapes and pictures. "I see them." I began transcribing the hieroglyphs that ran like carved tattoos down her legs.

The professor crouched over my shoulder. "It's an effigy to Princess Mapseti," he said with reverence.

I paused. "You know her?"

"There are several Mapsetis. Keep going."

I wrote as fast as I could.

His wide fingers hovered over the marks I'd made on the paper. "These are the princess's titles: daughter of Atwayum, keeper of the flame."

I could feel the excitement vibrating from my old teacher.

"Try the next statue," he said. Without question, I moved to the center statue, bypassing the mummy completely. He grew breathless as I copied the text as fast as I could. "Sesska," he exclaimed when I'd drawn the last symbol.

"What does that mean?" I asked.

He knelt next to me. "Move to the third."

He was going too fast. "I didn't get the titles for Sesska."

"It's okay. If the next one is Tuekennet..." he began, positively giddy.

I scooted to the third statue.

"Three divine ancestors guard the lost queen," he said over my shoulder.

I couldn't write fast enough for him or for me as I copied the last of the markings. This name was longer and I was afraid I was getting sloppier as I frantically transcribed. Professor Grassino, who usually prized neat student assignments, didn't mind a bit.

"Tuekennet." He sat back on his heels, eyes closed. "The last of the three ancestors who guard Queen Ephseti." He wiped a tear from the corner of his eye. "I knew she existed. I knew it!" He let out a small laugh. "We all knew it."

"We had a queen in the house," I said, gazing at the blackened remains of her body that showed through where the wrappings had been pulled away.

"Not just a queen." The professor ran a hand over his bald head. "The lost queen. Her son cursed her remains. He tried to wipe out her memory. We could never prove she existed. There were rumors her tomb had been found a century ago, but its contents never surfaced. Nobody knew who discovered her or what happened to the find."

"It was in my house," Lee said from the doorway, shocked.

"Oh, my good sir," the professor said, giddy as he leapt up and embraced Lee. "This is a day for the history books."

"We can search the house," Lee said. "If it's here, we'll find it."

"There were so many artifacts," I said, "jewelry and statues scattered on tables around the room."

"Set up for an unveiling." The professor nodded, his gaze roving the room as if trying to picture it. "Very common in that day."

Until tragedy struck the family.

Lee gasped as the air chilled. A long shadow, dark as night, slunk from the ceiling, down the wall, and across the floor toward the mummy. It was darker than before, stronger.

"It's going for the queen," I said, pointing to it. "Does anyone see it?"

Lee shook his head, eyes wide.

"Let's see what happens," the professor said, moving close to where the ghostly mummy lay, with absolutely no regard for the approaching danger.

I took a risk and followed him. "Look, I've done this before. Trust me when I tell you it isn't safe to stay here." I looked into his pale blue eyes and willed him to still have the same respect and affection for me when I said, "It is my professional opinion that this house and any treasure we find inside it could very well be cursed."

"Verity—" he began, with that tone he got when a student insisted that the city of Alexandria was on the Nile or that our beloved Ole Miss football team might not win that weekend. "You've convinced me on the ghosts. I admit that. But now you're talking hoodoo voodoo."

"Okay. You're right." I had gotten carried away. "I'm not so sure about dark magic curses, either. But I do believe in evil entities that can harm us," I told him.

He hesitated, then sighed. "I see your point," he admitted.

"People died in this house," I said. "Tragically. There's something dark and sinister behind those deaths. You know what happened to Jack Treadwell. I think it had something to do with this find."

He nodded. "Then let's take a look at his journals."

"All right." It made sense to try.

Who was I kidding? It made more sense to leave. But if we fled, like Robert urged, we'd never discover what really happened or be able to help.

I led the men out of the room and watched over my shoulder as the dark entity followed us to the doorway before sinking back into the floor.

CHAPTER 10

"THE JOURNALS SHOULD TELL US where they discovered the tomb," Professor Grassino said, striding through the haunted house like he owned it. "I'd love to put together an expedition, just in case there's anything left."

"This way," Lee said, as eager as I was to get out of the music room.

The professor whistled to himself as we made our way across the main floor. He had truly found his calling. I only hoped to be as lucky someday.

"Have you always seen ghosts?" he asked as we passed through the foyer.

"No," I said, distinctly uncomfortable as I stepped past the outline of Robert's dead body on the floor. The ghost had truly believed we were in danger. "I trapped a ghost on my property here in town, and he gives me the power to see other ghosts."

"Frankie the dead gangster helps her as long as she carries his urn and lets him visit places," Lee added.

The professor, who never missed a thing, stopped just outside the Egyptian room. "Is he here now?"

"I left him at home," I said. "He had things to do, so he just lent me his power this time." It sounded goofy, even to my ears. But after what I'd just shown Professor Grassino, I could probably tell him I tuned into the spirit world using my dollar-store hoop earrings and he'd believe me.

The professor was immediately distracted when we entered the room with the Egyptian games and decorations. "This is a real pique board." He smiled. "Clearly carved by hand."

"Is it an artifact?" Lee asked, letting down his guard a bit.

"Not in the way you're thinking," the professor said, sizing it up. "You see right here, where the legs meet the base…"

I moved ahead to the study and was startled to find Jack Treadwell sitting at his desk.

The mustached gentleman held a glass in his hand and stopped mid-drink when he saw me. "I hope I'm not interrupting," I said.

The ghost got over his surprise rather quickly and held up his glass to me. "Hell, these days, I'm glad for any company I can get."

"You're Jack Treadwell, famous archaeologist," I said, laying it on a bit thick.

It couldn't hurt.

The ghost smiled. "Don't let my wife see you in that dress."

My hand immediately went to my bare neck and upper chest. By today's standards, this morning's sundress was quite proper— white with blue hydrangeas. In fact, it was the fanciest I owned (and the only clean one). "I'm not from your era," I explained quickly. "In fact, I'm here to help you and your family recover from…what happened to you." I took a step closer. "You realize you're—"

"Dead at my desk?" he provided, resting his booted feet up on the polished wooden surface. "You can say it."

"I ran into Robert a little while ago," I ventured.

Jack arched his brows in surprise. "You don't say. That sod didn't even come to my funeral."

He said it fondly, which confused me. "Robert died a few days after you did." Jack probably hadn't been buried at that point.

"That's terrible," Jack said, taken aback.

"I ran into him out in the foyer," I said. "I'm surprised you haven't seen him."

The ghost frowned. "I don't see anyone. I hear things," he said, glancing around him. "I hear a woman crying."

"I think that's your wife, Annabelle."

"No," he insisted, unwilling to believe it. "She isn't here. If she was, she'd come to me."

Then something was holding her back. "I've seen her and your brother."

Jack gave no reaction.

Darn. It wasn't as if I could show him his family.

Perhaps Annabelle was too grief-stricken to reach out. As for Jack's brother? "Robert may be afraid to come into the study, on account of the curse. Do you get out much?"

Jack waved a hand. "There's no curse."

"Then can you tell me exactly what went wrong?"

He took his feet down and rested his elbows amid the scattered books and papers. "Damned if I know," he said, taking another drink.

"Would you mind if my friends and I took a look at the journals from your last dig? Your grandson is with me, as well as an archaeologist."

He stood. "You don't say?" He made quick work navigating the stacks of books around his desk. "Is he a famous archaeologist?" he asked, looking past me out the door. "The unveiling is this Saturday!"

"That would have been more than a hundred years ago," I said gently.

"Damn. That's right." I watched him deflate. "I was really looking forward to that."

I approached him cautiously. "Do you know where the queen's artifacts are?"

He gave me a look like I was daft. "In the music room. You can't miss them." He sighed. "I wish I'd discovered a king instead of a queen."

"Believe me, you did good. Where did you find the tomb?"

He held up his glass. "You'll have to wait for the unveiling."

The poor ghost seemed to be living more in the past than the present. "Please. Tell me what happened to you." I touched my fingertips to the cold, carved wood doorway. "I'd like to help your family find peace."

Treadwell shrugged and turned back to his desk. "My family is all gone." He shook his head. "I came home. They were so glad to see me. I was this close"—he pinched his fingers—"to unveiling my first big find." He passed straight through his desk and dropped into his chair. "Then I died and they abandoned me." He shook his head and reached for another drink.

I ran a hand along the door frame, wishing I could comfort him. "Your family is still here," I said gently.

He gave a humorless smirk. "I don't see any of them."

A shadowy figure crackled into view behind the ghost. For all I knew, it could be a part of him, his dark side—or even the thing that killed him. "Jack, what is that?"

He turned to see. "Trouble," he said.

"Wait—" I called as Jack's image faded.

I ducked out of the room faster than a hummingbird on a string and ran straight into Lee.

He caught me. "Are you all right?"

"You look like you've seen a ghost," the professor said jovially.

But Lee understood. "There is a malicious presence in this house," he said, staying close to us. "I've felt it for years and I don't have any special abilities. That's why I never came inside. And it's why I brought Verity with me when I even thought about walking through that front door."

"I just met the ghost of Jack Treadwell in that room," I said. "Your grandfather is doing well," I told Lee. He was family, after all. "But he wasn't able to tell me where he found the tomb or where the artifacts are now."

None of the ghosts had offered the help I'd expected. I was usually so good at drawing them out.

It was clear Jack didn't understand what had happened to him. I found it interesting that he didn't interact with any of the other ghosts in the house, but he had recognized the dark presence. Perhaps it had killed him.

"Well, let's take a look at those journals," the professor said, entering the study.

"Be careful," I warned, following him. "Whatever it was that I saw in the music room just made an appearance. There," I said, pointing to the area behind the messy desk. I saw no sign of it now. In all fairness, it would be hard to detect Lucy dyed pink in this place.

Lee eyed the door. "These are my grandfather's journals from the 1910 expedition," he said, showing the professor the set of leather-bound books we'd found.

"The expedition crates upstairs arrived in the United States on June 22, 1910," I added.

Professor Grassino searched for a bit and located the journal marked May 1910. "Let's see where they were digging," he said, opening the book. He scanned the pages for several minutes. "Hmm..."

"What?" I asked, sharing a glance with Lee.

The professor's finger moved down the page. "Just a second."

Lee peered at the book over the professor's shoulder.

I didn't feel too comfortable getting distracted in this room, so I kept watch while the men gave intermittent gasps.

"He's cagy with the location," the professor said. "Let's look at April."

"Over here, I think." Lee moved a stack of books to reveal three small stone jars on the shelf behind them. They looked like ancient Egyptian funerary relics.

"Well, would you look at that..." the professor said. "The mummy's organs would be kept in jars just like these."

"Are those from the queen's tomb?" I asked.

"It's hard to say." The professor reached for the one on the end.

"Wait," I said, "if there is a curse—"

Too late. He gently turned the jar with the head of a jackal.

"This could be dangerous," I finished. Not that I believed in ancient spells guarding a mummy's possessions, or magic hexes that bug-zapped you if you touched anything. But I did believe in vengeful ghosts. I'd met a few.

"No name on the jar that I can see. That's not unusual." He

fixed his gaze on me. "Who was this?" he asked, as if we were back in class.

And just like then, my brain scrambled a bit for the answer. "Duamutef. Jackal-headed god of the east," I said quickly, glad my old friend didn't appear any worse for wear.

So far so good. Maybe Robert's warning had made me paranoid. Or maybe the dark presence was merely biding its time.

"Good," the professor said, pleased at my ability to recall my studies. He turned back to the artifact. "This appears to be genuine. See the ancient carving marks?"

He was enjoying this.

I had to admit it was neat. I lobbed a grin at Lee, who seemed quite confused. "Those are the gods on canopic jars," I said to him.

"Now who else do we have over there?" Professor Grassino asked me.

"Qebehsenuef," with the head of the falcon. "Hapi," with the head of the baboon. "Where's Imseti?" I asked. There were always four jars, with the same four gods.

"I'm looking," the professor said, moving stacks of papers and books.

"I'll help," Lee said. He reached for the books on the high shelves, stacking them neatly on the floor, leaving no volume unturned.

"I don't see it in there," I told him, checking inside a box of maps.

"Whether or not these are from the tomb of the lost queen, this is a hugely significant historical find. I can guarantee you every museum in the country will want it."

"I don't know if I could sell it," Lee said, shooting me an apologetic glance. "This is my heritage."

"Good. With private collectors, you have no control over how the artifacts are kept," the professor said, handing another stack of books to Lee. "It's much better to sign contracts for the collection to go on tour. If it's complete, and if we can prove it is most likely from the lost queen's tomb, I'm talking high five-figure exhibition fees."

"I could hire people to restore the house and the gardens," Lee said on an exhale, as if we'd already completed the collection.

"I'll put you in contact with the right people." He clapped Lee on the back. "You'll be set."

So would I. At least, I'd certainly prove myself as a ghost hunter. And perhaps bring my finances into the black.

We just needed a bit more time to investigate.

Through the large window behind the desk, I saw Ovis raise his camera and take a picture.

"Stop it," I called while trying to block the large bay window. I had as much of a chance of stopping Ovis as I had at getting Frankie to fix me a steak dinner and tuck me in tonight. "Hide the jars," I said as Ovis aimed his camera straight at them.

Too late.

Ovis lowered the camera with a grin.

"We're sunk." The last thing we wanted was a front-page splash about treasure that people could steal...or the status of my first in-progress job as a ghost hunter.

"Not necessarily," the professor said, waving at Ovis. "You might need that reporter. He's excited about Jack's find and this house." He turned to Lee. "We do need to keep the details quiet while we search for the last jar and while I personally approach some key individuals, but generating public excitement is never a bad thing. I'll bet he could convince his editor to run a lot of stories if we succeed in this quest of ours. You just have to control the message."

"You met Ovis, right?" Lee asked.

I understood what he meant. "Ovis is more tenacious than a tick on a hound dog, and there's no way to control him once he gets an idea in his head."

The professor grinned and fiddled with the lid on a bottle of MacKinlay's scotch whiskey on the cocktail cart. "This is nice." He jiggled the cork and sniffed.

The bottle had been opened, which made sense. "Jack's ghost was drinking that."

"He has good taste. Even before it was hundred-and-twenty-year-old scotch," Lee said as the professor paused for Ovis to take a photo.

I trusted the professor. I did. But I also worried that he didn't understand how being in a haunted house—someone else's house—complicated things.

He winked at me, misunderstanding my hesitation. "Believe me. I've dealt with reporters before. Half of professorship is politics." He grinned at us. "I'll show you what to do."

"I'm in," Lee said. Of course he was—he needed money to save the property. But he hadn't seen what I had or heard Robert's warning.

The professor nodded. "The first thing we need to do with that reporter is buy more time. We want to prove we have the queen and be able to give the location of her tomb before we announce."

"I think I know a way to stall him," Lee said. He motioned to Ovis, who was still taking pictures of us from outside, and pointed toward the front door. "I'll need your help, Verity," he said, heading toward the front of the house.

"If you open that door, Ovis is coming in," I warned as we zigzagged past two couches and a Victrola in the parlor.

"The professor has a point. Media coverage could help, but we'll do it on my terms," he said. "A lot like what you did with your ghost story."

"I hate to tell you, but that didn't exactly work out."

But it seemed Lee was more of a doer than a thinker. He opened the door and, true to my prediction, Ovis nearly fell inside.

"You can enter," Lee said, too late. "Off the record, we're investigating ghosts and we located some interesting Egyptian artifacts."

"I knew it!" Ovis said, straightening, looking past us as if we had it all lined up, ready for him to document. "And you can't just say 'off the record,' I have to agree to it," he added, snapping a picture of the staircase, whistling at the size of the foyer.

"You can photograph anything you see in here," Lee said. "You print a spread of the house no one has seen in a generation. You can even write about Verity ghost hunting here, if she agrees."

Ovis looked to me. "I don't see where I have a choice," I said. Whoever had gifted the peach pie had probably told half the county by now.

"But no artifacts," Lee said. "Yet. When we know what we have, you get the exclusive. Otherwise, a newspaper article could spell trouble for our whole investigation."

"Agreed," Ovis said, shaking Lee's hand, dropping it almost immediately to take a shot of the grand staircase. "This place is fantastic." He moved past us to photograph the fireplace in the parlor before catching sight of the room full of antique board games. "You need to get an alarm system in here. And a guard." He edged in for a close-up shot of the pique board. "You ever think about selling some of this stuff?"

Lee frowned. "I'd have to empty the house in order to preserve it. Then where would we be?" Exhibiting the artifacts was a better idea if we could make it work.

"Vera's great-grandmother used to play here as a kid. Before... damn," he muttered to himself, taking a shot of a half-burned cigar still in an ashtray on the mantel.

"You really think you can control the story?" I murmured to Lee.

"For now," he said, watching Ovis move toward the study. He was making quick work of documenting every detail of the foyer, probably afraid we'd change our minds and toss him out. "I know we didn't anticipate involving Ovis."

"It's okay," I told him. It was my fault anyway.

For having a private conversation in my kitchen of all places.

"Don't take any more pictures of the jars," Lee said, heading to intercept the reporter as he entered the study.

Ovis let out a cry. "Somebody call 911!"

We rushed into the room to find the reporter behind the desk, crouched over the prone body of Dale Grassino lying facedown on the floor. Ovis rolled him over, and the professor lay with his jaw slack, his gaze glassy and unresponsive.

Worse, I saw shards of white and silver light glittering above him. They were soul traces, which told me beyond a doubt that we'd lost him.

CHAPTER 11

WE CALLED THE PARAMEDICS AND Ovis drove as we followed the ambulance to the ER. On the way, I dialed the professor's sister, who had been an emergency contact when I used to house-sit for him. She said she'd head over.

I'd neglected to even ask her exactly where she lived or how long she'd take to get here. No matter. I'd stay until she arrived.

There had been no way to tell her on the phone that her brother had already passed. It seemed wrong when I couldn't tell her how I'd come to know, that Frankie's power had allowed me to see proof.

From the moment we arrived at the ER, Lee couldn't sit still. He and Ovis went to grab a coffee in the cafeteria and maybe walk a bit outside.

I took a seat in the waiting room and, for a few minutes at least, had the place to myself.

The wide, rectangular room was done in beige and gray, with pink and gray cloth chairs of an indeterminate age. I ran a finger over the paintbrush-swipe pattern on my seat cushion and wondered if this had ever been in style outside of hospitals and doctors' offices.

I should have listened to Robert's warning. I should have pointed to the smoking spot on the floor and told the professor and Lee that we had to get out of there.

I folded my hands in my lap. The paramedics had suspected

a heart attack, but I didn't buy it. This was a man who ran half-marathons for fun and excavated stone tombs in hot countries every summer. Not that he couldn't be struck down by health issues like anyone else, but why today? And why in the study of Rock Fall manor, where Jack Treadwell had also had his heart attack?

No. I'd brought Dale Grassino to Rock Fall. I'd witnessed the strength of Robert's warning. I'd seen the dark presence right behind that desk, and I'd let the professor investigate the journals anyway.

"It's my fault," I whispered. Saying it out loud made me feel worse, but that was the point. I had to face the truth and somehow take responsibility for my actions.

I detected motion to my left and saw a nurse glide straight through the wall beside a rack of magazines. Dang it. It had quite slipped my mind that I still had Frankie's power.

The sturdy woman wore a crisp white dress and an angular nurse's cap. Her silver hair curled in a practiced wave that suggested she was more at home in the 1940s.

She gave me a small smile and I fought the urge to sigh. As pleasant as she seemed, I wasn't in the mood. I didn't want to see any ghosts right now, not even the professor's, and he would be in a transition stage for months if not years.

And as much as I wanted to see the professor again, to apologize, how horrible it would be to see him in spirit form when he died helping me. Assuming he even came back, which most ghosts didn't. I tried to think of something else.

The ghostly nurse hovered into my line of vision again. I did my best to look straight through her, like I didn't see anything. Maybe she'd leave me alone.

It wasn't like I could go anywhere. I'd told the professor's sister I'd be here.

Instead of taking the hint, the ghost eased into the seat next to me. Out of the corner of my eye, I could see her white-stockinged knee, her hands folded patiently in her lap, the deep lines in her face.

She caught me watching her. "You can see me."

"Yes," I said. But if I could take it all back, I would.

Her expression softened. "Sometimes just sitting with someone helps." She leaned back and relaxed in the chair, as if she needed the support. "Whatever happened...you can't blame yourself." She had no idea. "I brought my friend to a dangerous place." A cursed place. And then he went and handled those relics—just like Jack. Of course he did. He was a hands-on professor in class and direct in every one of his excavations. I should have known that would cause trouble.

I would have if I hadn't been so eager to make sense of the goings-on in that house to prove that I could make it as a ghost hunter.

"We all make mistakes," she said, as if we had something in common. And now I'd done the one thing I'd attempted to avoid—I'd let her engage with me. I'd blazed forward without thinking. Again. She acted like us sitting here, having our little talk, was the most natural thing in the world. "Do you think your friend would blame you?" she asked, as if she really wanted to know.

The answer was simple, of course. "He's not that way." He'd never want me to feel bad. "He'd just say it was an accident." One with terrible consequences.

Her expression softened. "If he wouldn't blame you, do you think he'd want you to hurt yourself like this?"

I scooted forward in my chair and rested my elbows on my knees. She had a point.

"Thanks," I said. I glanced over at her, so serene in her chair. And, hey, at least there was one new ghost willing to talk to me. "Did you work here?" I asked.

The corner of her mouth quirked. "Eighty-three years next month."

"You realize you're..." I wasn't sure if she was as sensitive as Frankie about the word *dead*.

"I understand I don't live and breathe in the medical sense. It's okay." She shrugged a shoulder. "I can still do a lot of good."

"You have," I told her. "Thank you."

She nodded and then she simply sat with me so I wouldn't be alone as the minutes ticked by. I'm not sure how long we sat that way before Ellis walked into the room, with an expression that made me fear the worst.

He wore his tan and black deputy sheriff's uniform and rested a hand on his gun belt as he moved to sit next to me.

"Not there," I said, blocking the nurse's seat.

He didn't question. Instead, he drew me to my feet and folded me into a hug. "I'm sorry, Verity."

"He's gone," I said.

Ellis pulled away to look at me. He tucked a lock of hair behind my ear, his fingers lingering on my cheek. "Do you want to see him?"

"No." That moment in the study had been enough.

"His sister is in there with him. She arrived a few minutes ago."

She must have gone straight back.

A man cleared his throat nearby. Detective Duranja stood near the entrance to the waiting room, clearly uncomfortable. "I told Lee I'd give him a ride home," he said to Ellis and to me. "We're done with his statement," Duranja added. "Is there anything else?"

"I'll take care of Verity's statement," Ellis said quickly, dismissing the other officer.

"Statement?" I reclaimed the chair I'd used before.

Ellis crouched in front of me. "911 dispatch called us in," he said, "since the circumstances were unusual."

"Sure." Old house. Dead archaeologist. Definitely unusual— but perhaps not for Rock Fall.

"We questioned Lee outside. He gave us the basics on why Professor Grassino was there and what you saw. Ovis gave the same account."

"All right. I'll give you mine." I ran through the incident at the house, and Ellis nodded, not surprised by any of it.

He glanced back to make sure we were truly alone. "Now

what else happened?" he asked pointedly. He meant on the spiritual side.

That was the million-dollar question.

"I can't say for sure." I told him about the discovery in the music room and about the canopic jars and how my professor couldn't keep his hands off them.

"We found one near the body," Ellis said. "We think he'd been handling it."

"Don't touch it," I warned him.

"Don't worry. The jar is evidence. Nobody's directly in contact with it." At my sigh of relief, he shifted his stance. "Maybe Professor Grassino's death had nothing to do with the house," he said unconvincingly.

I shot him a look.

He glanced away. "You gotta admit a curse sounds crazy."

It did. "But you know better." He'd experienced all kinds of crazy with me.

He turned back to me. "Okay. The question is what do we do about it?"

I stood, knees a bit shaky. It was my job to figure that out. "I'm going back into the house." It was the best way I could think of to find out what really happened. I owed Professor Grassino that. "I'll talk to the ghosts." I'd find a way to make real contact. "There are still rooms on the first floor I haven't searched, not to mention the basement."

"Most of those houses near the rock cliffs don't have basements," Ellis said.

"Good." I really didn't want to go down in one.

In any case, I'd find the missing canopic jar. If it was still on the property. I'd just have to be careful. If the professor hadn't died of natural causes, then something in the house was much more dangerous than we'd ever realized.

Ellis rose and took my arm to steady me. "I'm going in with you."

"It's not safe," I said, not sure I wanted to involve anyone else I cared about.

"At least it's not a haunted speakeasy full of dead gangsters," he said, referring to another one of our adventures. "Talk about not feeling welcome."

"Just because they shot at us?" I asked, letting him walk me out. "It was better than the time we got buried alive."

"You always know how to make a guy feel brave," he quipped, shaking me out of my funk. "I'll get us in there tomorrow after the investigation team is finished. In the meantime, let's get you home." We passed the ghost nurse from the waiting room on the way out. She kept company with an older man, still living, who sat in a wheelchair near the registration desk. I gave her a small wave, and she smiled. "Ovis had a friend of his bring your car up," Ellis continued, "but I told him you might not want to drive."

"Ovis did that?" I asked as we headed through the sliding glass doors to the circle drive. Sure enough, the land yacht stood waiting in the front row of the parking lot next to the ER.

"He's always thinking six steps ahead," Ellis said.

Ellis's squad car was parked in the circle. The sun had set. The air felt warm and comforting. And there was nothing I wanted more than to slip into that car and let him handle the rest of my night.

But I couldn't do it. Not yet. "You know what? I think I will drive myself home. I have some things I need to deal with."

If I let Ellis drive me, I'd end up back at his place instead of mine. And while Ellis's house would be a welcome sanctuary, I wasn't making things up when I said I had more to do tonight.

If my suspicions were correct, my good friend Frankie had created a gangster paradise in my lovely sanctuary of a backyard. And now that I had his power, I was going to see exactly what he was trying to pull.

Ellis followed me out of the lot, but I lost him on the highway. No doubt he'd head back to the station to hear the report on the situation at Rock Fall mansion.

I was done with it, at least for today. I'd already given too much.

I had my purse. I still had the doll stashed in the backseat of my car. Anything else would resolve itself tomorrow.

Highway 4 took me back into town, and I eased off of it onto Rural Route 9. The hills and turns along the narrow country road made for slower driving, but they forced me to think about the road and not about the horrible scene I'd witnessed at the mansion.

Trees stretched over the blacktop from both sides, blocking out the moon and turning my headlights into two distinct circles of light stretching to oblivion.

I wondered what Rock Fall mansion would be like in the dark.

Goose bumps prickled along my arms. *It doesn't matter. You're not going back there tonight.*

I needed to focus on what was real: The ribbon of blacktop stretching out in front of me. The quiet of the night.

I adjusted my rearview mirror and saw the little ghost girl sitting in my backseat, clutching her doll.

Sweet Jesus!

I slammed on the brakes, the back of the car fishtailing wide as I wrestled it to a stop. There was no shoulder. My car sat half-on, half-off a strip of gravel as I forced myself to turn around and face the ghost in my backseat.

But she was gone. The seat sat empty.

The doll lay on her side, smiling.

CHAPTER 12

I DROVE THE REST OF THE way home with both eyes wide open and a hand over my heart.

Multiple, frenetic glances in my rearview mirror showed no more visits from the girl in my backseat. No traffic behind me either.

Drive.

I crested a hill on the rural roadway, my lights illuminating the blacktop in front of me, unable to cut into the darkness beyond.

The little girl had appeared back there for a reason. Maybe she'd decided to talk, and my panic had driven her away. Perhaps she'd only wanted her doll. If so, why had she given it to me in the first place? And why didn't she take it back with her?

The only thing I knew was that my land yacht had become the creepiest place in six counties.

I hit the gas, testing the engine and my tolerance for breaking the speed limit as I hauled butt back to my place.

My fingers ached from gripping the wheel as I steered up the long drive toward home. It felt like I'd been gone a week.

I let out a long sigh as I caught sight of my lovely old house, with its front porch light as welcoming as a fresh batch of biscuits. Home at last. I needed to get out of this car and into a nice, hot bathtub—with every door locked behind me.

As if that would keep out a ghost.

I steered the car toward my favorite parking spot in the back of the house and was shaken out of my homespun reverie when I heard laughter, jazz music, and the unmistakable din of a party in progress.

Because, of course, I'd left Frankie in charge.

Ghostly whiskey bottles littered my backyard.

"Darn it, Frankie." I slammed a hand on my steering wheel. I could hardly park my car among the several dozen ghostly gangsters drinking and dancing in my backyard.

Somehow, I managed to find a spot. And when I stepped out of the car, I saw wiseguys splashing in the cozy fishing pond beyond my favorite apple tree…naked!

"That's it!" I grabbed my bag from the seat, leaving the freaky doll in the back. "Where's Frankie?" I asked the drunken flapper dancing in circles next to my front bumper.

She giggled and spilled half a glass of champagne on my hood. She blew a kiss at me and pointed toward my back porch.

A jazz band struck up a hard beat next to my hummingbird feeder and I saw the traitor to the right of two trumpet players. Along with the band, they'd somehow managed to cram my porch full of a half-dozen gambling stations. Frankie stood at the head of a craps table, throwing dice to the cheers of his friends.

"Swell party!" the flapper said, holding up her glass for a mock toast, nearly spilling the rest of the drink on her head.

"The fun's over," I said, storming up the back steps, past a blond gangster with a lock of hair that fell stylishly over his forehead. Dimestore Bobby. He winked at me.

Suds leaned against the porch post at the top of the stairs and pulled the half-smoked cigar from his lips. "It's all legal," he said, hefting a bottle, "except for the gin. Wait." He spread his arms. "That's legal now, too!"

"Joy to the world," I said, barreling past the gangster. Suds had been stuck in a tunnel, dead, for a good part of this century. I felt for him, but not enough to sacrifice my home and my sanity.

And how had so many ghosts died with so much gambling equipment?

"Frankie," I demanded as I scooted past a rowdy poker table, trying to ignore the couple making out on my porch swing.

"Whoa! Hey!" the crowd at the table cheered.

A smiling Frankie raised both hands and accepted high fives and slaps on the back for his win. He appeared as if he didn't have a worry in the world.

"You fix this," I warned him.

He stacked a wad of ghostly cash on the pass line. "I, for one, am rather shocked that you care."

Baloney. "You hid this from me." He hadn't turned on my ghost-seeing abilities this morning until I was well away from the backyard.

Frankie stepped out from behind the table. The entire lower section of his body was missing from the waist down. "You drained half my energy today," he said, dropping the cute act. "I'm half gone to heck." He looked down past his fading waist-line. "I can't even go skinny-dipping looking like this."

"You don't get it." None of them did. "You and your obnoxious friends are taking over," I bit off. "This is my home!"

"And this is my life!" he shouted.

I stared at him. Frankie never yelled, at least not about anything so personal.

He straightened his tie and cleared his throat. "All I'm saying is you should be happy you're not paying for the band." He dug into his coat pocket and handed off a stack of cash to Suds. "That should do us till morning."

I felt bad about his afterlife, and his lower half. But we had to be reasonable. "You can *not* have a jazz band out here all night."

"Watch me," he said as his friend eyed us and counted the cash. "I'm on a hot streak a mile wide. If I keep shooting like this, we could be here for days." The gangsters at the table cheered, which only egged Frankie on. "Have you people ever seen so many sevens?" he called.

"He's nuts," I said to Suds.

"You always this square?" Suds asked me, around his stogie.

"Pay them," Frankie said, handing his friend a wad of dough. His friend gave a quick nod and headed off to do his bidding.

Frankie took up his dice again.

"This wasn't part of our agreement and you know it," I said.

He rattled the dice in his hand. "I'm going to take my power back in a minute," he said. "If you ever want to use it again, you're going to let me have my gang headquarters."

A dingbat flapper giggled and leaned in so close I had to twist sideways to avoid touching her. Frankie let her blow on his dice. She giggled and batted her lashes at him.

"So that's how it is," I huffed. I realized with a sinking feeling that I had no other argument.

He was right. We'd made a deal. Worse, I'd dictated the terms. I just hadn't anticipated exactly what it meant to have the gang over.

The flapper sized me up as if I were competition.

Not in this universe or any other. But I did need his power—now more than ever.

"All right," I said, gathering my dignity, "you can have your party."

Frankie grinned like the cat that ate the canary.

"Just don't disturb the neighbors," I added as I felt the unmistakable tingle of his power leaving me.

"They ain't invited," Frankie said, his energy rising out of my body with a crackle and a jolt.

The gambling table shimmered into nothingness. The flapper's high-pitched giggle faded, along with the sounds of the band and the party on the lawn and clinking of glasses.

Not a minute later, I stood in front of half-of-a-Frankie, on a perfect summer evening in Tennessee. Frankie tossed the dice again and they disappeared as soon as they left his hand. "Yes!" he said, tossing his arms up.

Another win, but this time, I didn't hear the cheers of the gambling crowd.

Insects buzzed and bullfrogs called to one another in the night.

I spotted my little skunk curled on the porch of all places. "Lucy," I called, hurrying over to her, hoping she hadn't been too afraid of the band.

"She's been hanging out all night under the poker table," Frankie groused.

"You're not scared?" I asked my girl as I lifted her up. She grunted and snuggled in my arms, but she wasn't upset. "Maybe she's okay with ghosts now." I turned her toward Frankie. "You might have won her over." But she took one look at him and started scrambling to get away. "Lucy!" I chided as she tried to climb my head. "Stop. It's okay." I caught her in my arms, trying to soothe her, but she was having none of it. "Huh," I said, glancing at the gangster.

He took off his hat and wiped the sweat from his brow. "Turns out she's okay with ghosts, she just doesn't like me."

"That's not true," I offered, stroking Lucy's ears as she scrambled in terror from the ghost in front of me.

"I don't know what I ever did," the gangster muttered, turning back to the invisible table that I'd seen only moments ago.

"I don't know either," I murmured to her, easing into the house and locking the door behind us, "but you do have good taste."

"I heard that," Frankie called from the porch.

"I need a soak," I said to the skunk, careful not to use the word *bath*. She knew that word and she always thought it was about *her*.

But I was the one in need of bubbles tonight. I'd met four ghosts at Rock Fall mansion, been scared out of my wits by all of them, dodged a dark shadow, found ghostly artifacts, and then some real ones that might have led to the death of my former professor. I poured the last glass of wine from a bottle Ellis and I had shared and retreated to the upstairs bathroom.

Lucy watched as I filled my claw-foot tub with olive blossom scented bath bubbles. Then she curled up on a towel next to the sink while I sipped on a crisp pinot and lowered myself into the steaming, fragrant water. I placed a warm washcloth over my eyes and leaned back all the way to bliss. Maybe soon, when Lee's cucumbers came in, I could cut a few to place on my eyes. It would be a regular spa up here.

Heaven knew I needed it.

Frankie had me over a barrel when it came to hosting the gang. I hadn't even liked crazy parties when I was in college, much less now. Still, I didn't see a way out of it. Not unless I could find them another place on my property.

I did own the bit of land past the fishing pond. Maybe we could finagle a gang headquarters for the South Town boys out there. Nothing permanent, of course.

Maybe Ellis could help me build a shed...

I reached for my wineglass, and my fingertips came in contact with a glossy surface that didn't feel at all like my drink. Smooth, rounded, and very, very cold. I lifted the washcloth off my eyes and saw that I held the smiling face of the doll in the purple dress.

CHAPTER 13

I DIDN'T SLEEP MUCH THAT NIGHT. Even after I returned the doll to the backseat of my car. Even after Frankie offered up Suds as a bodyguard.

I mean, we were talking about a little girl. True, she was a creepy one that seemed to be able to move objects in a way I'd never experienced before. But having Suds here wasn't the answer. I didn't want any ghosts watching me sleep, not now—not ever.

Which was why I lay flat on my back, covers to my chin on my futon in the parlor, with every light blazing, in case the ghost of the little girl happened to pop up when I least expected her.

Next to me, Lucy stretched out on her back, her furry body forming a perfect half circle. She snored lightly, her belly exposed. She had no worries.

Outside, Frankie gave another victory whoop at the craps table.

How had so many ghosts invaded my personal space in such a short amount of time? And why did the gangsters on the back porch seem like the least threatening of the bunch?

I slept late the following morning and woke near noon with a skunk pawing at my face.

"Lucy," I protested, batting her away, which only encouraged her to jump onto my chest.

She was heavier than she looked, a solid ten-pound bowling

ball. She grunted and a cold wet nose hit my ear, signaling in no uncertain terms that breakfast was long overdue.

We'd never slept this late before.

"I'm up," I groaned, scooting her onto the cushion next to me and sitting as best I could.

She hit me with a well-aimed nose to the elbow that I took to mean, "You're not up fast enough, sweetie. And it's not nice to starve a skunk."

I made her a blueberry salad topped with Vita-Skunk and arranged another plate of berries for myself.

"Come along," I said, holding the back door open for her. Gray clouds stretched overhead and the remnants of a morning rain dripped from the trees.

There was no sign of Frankie.

We ate breakfast out on the porch swing, to the chirps of birds and the rustling of leaves in the breeze. "This is how it *should* be," I said, biting into a sweet berry while Lucy, nose down, scarfed her breakfast.

It was hard to believe I'd seen a gangster party out here last night. But it had been real. As real as the death of my poor professor yesterday. In my mind's eye, I could see the white swirling light of Professor Grassino's soul traces, the last bit left behind by his spirit as he departed this earth.

I needed to learn what had happened to him and how to bring peace to the ghosts in that house. I suspected both had something to do with the dark spirit I'd seen. It was my moral obligation to put an end to this before anyone else got hurt—or killed.

Lucy's bowl rattled as she pushed it around on the porch by my feet. "I think it's empty." She'd licked out the last of the berry juice and, now, she just had a bowl. "I'll make you more for supper." She sure loved Lee's produce.

I'd be certain to compliment him on it and perhaps secure a fresh basket for tonight.

I placed the dishes in the sink and grabbed my cell phone from the kitchen island. My sister, Melody, had called several times, no doubt worried when she heard the news about

Professor Grassino. I called her back to let her know I was all right, then put in a call to Lee.

His phone rang and rang, which was strange. We hadn't talked since arriving at the hospital last night. Certainly, we had plenty to say now. I eyed Lucy, who stood at my feet, tail swishing, no doubt hopeful for a refill on her blueberry salad.

"I'm worried," I told her. "I don't know why Lee's not answering his cell." He'd certainly want to talk to me after last night, and he didn't seem like the type to sleep the morning away.

I placed the phone back on the counter. "We'll give him a minute," I told her.

After I'd gotten ready for the day, I tried him again with no response.

All right. As soon as I found Frankie, I'd head over there.

I checked the back porch, then the rose garden, but there was no sign of Frankie. Perhaps last night's party had taken a lot out of him. He was probably in the ether, an in between realm that seemed to have more energy than earth. It was where he liked to rest sometimes. But I'd give the yard a good look-see, just in case.

There was no sign of him under the apple tree. Or skinny-dipping in the pond, thank goodness.

Unless he'd freed himself by being happy.

I wasn't quite sure what to think about that, if it was even possible, when I detected movement in the field beyond. "Frankie?" I called, heading over to investigate. A semitransparent bent knee emerged from the tall grass. That was all I could see.

Too bad I'd sold the lawnmower.

Then a hand waved at me. The rest of the ghost lay prone.

"Is that you?" I asked, jogging out to him through the wet lawn.

I found him on his back, smiling. He'd lost his tie, his jacket, his shoes. At least he had his legs and feet back.

He'd undone the top three buttons of his shirt, revealing part of a surprisingly muscled chest. I'd never seen him this disheveled. "Baby cakes," he said, dropping his hand onto the ground by his head, "I had fun last night."

"I know, I was there." For at least part of it. "What brought you out this way?" I asked, following his gaze to the cloudy sky above. "Contemplating life?"

"Drag racing," he said with relish, reaching inside his shirt to scratch his chest. "I bought a car last night. A 1934 Riley MPH convertible. With a radio and a heater."

I didn't know if he was joking or not. He couldn't get cold anymore—or feel the wind in his hair. But he did like to control the radio. "I don't see any cars out here," I said, scanning the field. If it was on the ghostly plane, I wasn't sure if it would appear with Frankie or not. "How does that work?"

He sat up slowly. "Well," he said, drawing out the word, "Sticky Pete stole it out from under me. But he'll be back." He reached into his shirt pocket and pulled out a ghostly Rolex. "I lifted his watch."

We watched as it dissolved in his hand. "Dang. Pete's left the property." He shrugged. "Now I gotta steal it again."

This was what I'd invited into my life.

"At least you have all your parts back," I said, looking on the bright side.

He stood, shaking out his legs as he did. "I find I recover much faster when I'm having fun."

"That actually works out well, because I need you to come to the mansion. I'm worried about Lee."

He laughed. "That is not fun. This—" he spread his arms "this is where I'm meant to be."

Really? "Lying in a field at one o'clock in the afternoon."

"Pretty much," he agreed, running his fingers through his hair. "Besides, you want my friends to have free run of this place?"

"How many of them are still here?" I squinted, looking out over my peaceful backyard, as if that would help me see.

"A few. I mean, we did lose some. Crazy Sam doesn't like to be gone from the asylum too long. The Greely brothers haunt the highway. Suds is off robbing the liquor store. Last I saw, the band had passed out in the lake. No telling who else. It'd be impossible to clear them out, not if they don't want to leave. So if I did go with you, we'd have to leave Five Alarm Harry in charge."

It had been so much simpler with one ghost on my property. "Why do you call him Five Alarm Harry?"

"He likes to set fires," Frankie said, as if it were a hobby or something. "Big ones. Remember the great Nashville fire of 1916?"

I didn't know if he was warning me or joking. "You know what? Fine. You stay here." No doubt it was what he wanted anyway. "But I do need to borrow your power. I need to see what's really happening over at Rock Fall."

"Yeesh. You haven't given up on that place yet?"

"I never will."

Frankie listened to someone I couldn't see. "Yeah, I know she's got spunk. And she's quick." He eyed me. "She'd be real useful for the armored car heist."

"I didn't hear that, Frankie." I would not be an accessory to crime and they couldn't touch an armored car, anyway. They'd pass right through it and everything it contained. "Now lend me your power."

"Give, give, give…that's all I do," he said, walking toward the house, a bit unsteady on his feet. He motioned me to follow. "Let's head out front"—he glanced behind us—"since you don't want to see what we have cooking out here."

Because whatever they had going on at the moment was worse than drag racing in my field or skinny-dipping in my pond.

"Let me get my keys," I told him.

I fetched my purse from the house and made sure to lock Lucy inside, curled on her favorite blanket.

Frankie cringed when he saw the doll in the backseat of my car. I'd exiled it there after the bathtub incident.

I hesitated. "There's no way to make you feel better about this, is there?"

"Just drive," he said, keeping his eyes on the road.

I steered the land yacht out to the front of the house and

parked. "All right."

He glanced out the window, toward the rear of the house. "Drive a little more."

"Truly?" I transferred my foot to the gas and eased the car along the driveway.

"More," Frankie coaxed, almost to the end of my property.

"Now?" I asked when we'd reached the very edge.

Frankie made the iffy sign with his hand. "Beware of loud noises," he said, letting his power prickle over me.

A gunshot cracked behind the house, startling me.

"Told you," he said pragmatically.

"The house had better be standing when I get back," I said, only half joking.

He chuckled and floated out the door.

I told myself it didn't matter. I couldn't control the ghosts, not even the one who lived with me. I'd just have to trust Frankie and pray for the best.

In the meantime, I kept looking forward, toward the job I had to do and the ghosts I'd face at Rock Fall mansion.

Lee wasn't at the cottage when I pulled up a short time later. His garden behind the house stood deserted as well. Nothing of a ghostly nature stirred, which I supposed could be considered positive, except that I couldn't shake the feeling that something was wrong.

I hopped back in the car to try the mansion itself. It stood dark and forlorn under the cloudy sky.

Certainly, Lee wouldn't enter alone, especially after what had happened yesterday. I tried the door anyway. The wood rattled against the old lock, but didn't open.

I had to admit, I was a bit relieved. If I could have walked inside, I'd have felt obligated to search for Lee.

Alone.

"All right," I said, stepping back, keeping my gaze on the windows by the porch and on the empty yard beyond.

I ventured out back, past the half-dead hedgerows.

The remains of an expansive brick porch hunkered under a falling-down pergola. Weeds spilled out of rusted iron pots. Beyond, crumbling rock paths stretched out toward a round pool choked with vines and purple flowering weeds.

Beyond the pool, gnarled trees towered over life-sized statues of Greek goddesses, their faces turned to the sky or toward their water jugs, blissfully unaware of the vines snaked around their bodies, squeezing them like giant anacondas.

"Lee!" I called, passing under the shadows of the trees, trying to stick to the remains of the path.

If he was out here working, he could be hard to spot.

The trees broke. Straight ahead, I saw the fountain we'd visited on our first night in the gardens. I made a hard left, away from that place.

A low brick wall ran away from the clearing and I followed it toward a looming structure behind a copse of trees. When I drew closer, I saw it was an old carriage house. It stood two stories tall, with two pairs of arched wooden doors. Narrow windows squeezed in between, their shutters closed tight.

This might be a convenient place for Lee to keep his gardening tools. "Lee?"

The doors were locked tight, but I did spot a window with a shutter half falling off. Nearby, a naked smiling cherub had lost his head. It lay on the ground at his feet, so I borrowed it and placed it near the wall. Standing upon it, I could just see over the window ledge. When I tried to open the shutter all the way, it gave up its hold on the building and clattered to the ground.

"Whoops." Now I was kind of glad the owner hadn't answered my calls.

I peered in the window, through the rippled glass caked with dirt.

It seemed as if this building had stood abandoned for some time. It appeared on the ghostly plane as it did in real life. Large tires with white rims and honest-to-goodness spokes hung from hooks on the wall, as if waiting to be mounted onto the open-roofed, single-seat roadster parked inside. The next bay held a turn-of-the-century truck, with a boxy closed carriage. Hay bales, blackened with age, were stacked in the back. More hay bales crowded the small workbench to the right.

"You get a nice look?" a voice asked from behind me.

I spun and leapt off the cherub's head. "You scared me," I said, realizing I was addressing a handsome, dark-haired ghost. He held a pair of large garden shears and eyed me like he didn't quite know what to make of a girl standing on his statuary. "It was broken when I found it," I explained.

He made a helpless gesture with his free hand. "The whole place is falling apart. It's a shame."

"Do you work here?" I asked. His rough black pants and simple shirt seemed appropriate for a job outside, even if his vest didn't seem entirely practical.

"I'm in charge of the gardens." He glanced out over the ruined landscape. "Or I was."

"Verity Long," I said, by way of introduction.

"Tobias Crowe." He nodded. "I saw you the last time you were out here. You tell the Treadwell boy he's doing a fine job."

"Lee?" I asked. "Have you spotted him this morning?"

"Sure did. He was out by the gazebo. I'll show you," he said, gesturing for me to join him on the path. "I think he's getting ready to plant some blue lobelia, a fine choice," he said, his head passing through a low-lying tree limb.

I ducked around the overgrowth. "I'll bet you see a lot that goes on here," I offered.

He gave no reaction. "My focus was always on plants rather than people," he said diplomatically, "it makes life simpler."

Right now, I would have preferred a gossip. "Did you work here during the tragedy?"

We walked in silence for a few moments and I was afraid he wouldn't answer. "Jack's father, Hank Treadwell, hired me. He was an amateur botanist and spared no expense on his garden." He paused to look over a plant that had overgrown the path. "You tell Lee he's doing a good job. He reminds me a lot of

Hank in the way he cares for his plants. He takes the time to do things right."

I tried to see the garden as it once was, full of life and beauty. At least the birds still chirped. And animals scuttled through the underbrush.

"Were you here for the fire in the grape arbor?" I asked.

He dropped his eyes to the path. "They let us all go after the family died. But I heard about it. Happened right over there," he said, pointing to a tangled mess of weeds a short way from the carriage house. A ruined statue of Dionysus, the Greek god of wine, stood half-buried in the overgrowth. The muscled, bearded god held up a handful of grapes and a flagon of wine.

I stepped off the path, into the tangle of weeds, but I saw no other ghosts and no lingering evidence of fire damage in the overgrowth of wild bushes and weeds. "Is it true that the fire happened a month after the family's passing?"

He scratched his jaw. "That sounds about right."

Intrigued, I ran my feet along the ground, searching for...I didn't know what.

"You'd best stick to the path," Tobias warned. "We get snakes."

"I'll be careful," I called. Then my sole hit something hard.

The ghost frowned as I bent and dug out a half-buried iron candle plate poured in a floral pattern. Black wax collected in the grooves. Or it could be old wax gone black with age. "Do you know whose this is?" I asked, holding it out to him.

The gardener made a sign of the cross. "Leave it there."

"Did it belong to the governess?" I pressed. "The flowers appear to be jasmines. I smelled those in her room. She was out here when the arbor burned."

"I never gave her no mind," Tobias said, going defensive. "She was a strange one."

"I think I'll keep it." It would go nicely with my creepy doll. I'd keep all the pieces together, even if I didn't quite know what they meant yet.

"Leave it," Tobias instructed, gliding away from the ruined grape arbor. "It doesn't belong to you."

"True," I conceded. And I did want his help, and his company. Quickly, I placed the candleholder back where I found it, making note of its location so I could examine it again if need be.

A short distance away, under a copse of trees, I spotted an old graveyard. "Is this where the family is buried?" I asked, pushing farther into the garden.

Gnarled tree roots thrust from the soil, tripping me, and weeds rose up all around. Yet the small, fenced cemetery appeared tidy. The wrought-iron gate creaked as I pushed through and stepped onto perfectly manicured grass. I saw the rounded graves of Jack and Annabelle and a smaller stone for Charlotte. Robert's stood a distance away, stark in its simplicity.

"Lee keeps it up nice," Tobias said, hovering near the more modern, flat grave of Jack Junior. "Lee came back to Sugarland because it was his father's wish to be buried here. Annabelle begged Jack Junior to come home after Jack's death. He took the next train from New York. By the time he got to town, there were two policemen waiting for him at the station. Told him his mother was dead and his sister. They thought someone was targeting the family. Told him to turn around and go back to New York."

I crouched low and ran a hand over his cold grave. "How awful for him." To be separated from his family like that when they needed him most. "Did the authorities ever tell him it was safe to return?"

"Even if they had, what was left to return to?" Tobias asked. "His family was dead and buried. He stayed in New York until it was time for him to be buried with them."

"How sad. And then Lee moved into the gardener's house. Is Jack Junior here in spirit?"

Tobias shook his head. "I've never seen him."

"What about the governess? She stayed. Is she buried here?"

"She is," he said quietly. "They didn't give her a tombstone, but she's right over there," he said, pointing to a narrow plot a small distance away from the family.

Good. At least she had a place. "I'm told she was found in the kitchen. Do you know how she died?"

He glided away through the fence and into the trees. "That's enough gossip."

"Wait for me." I said a quick prayer for the departed and rushed to join the ghost.

He'd made it all the way to the path beyond the overgrown orchard by the time I caught up with him. I knew I was trying his patience, but I needed his help.

"I'm sorry to impose, but it is important we speak," I explained. "Lee asked me to help figure out what's going on in the house and gardens," I added, fighting off the gnats.

"Nothing that a bit of elbow grease won't fix," the ghost muttered, his eyes straight ahead.

If only it were so simple. "We're looking for an artifact inside that could help Lee gain the financial resources to fix up the estate."

Tobias shoved his hands into the pockets of his work pants. "I don't know about any of that," he said, glancing at the mansion, leading me toward the fountain where Lee and I had seen the doll heads. "I don't go anywhere near that house."

I took a chance and pressed harder. "Is it because of the dark presence inside?"

"I belong out here," he said, as if that answered anything.

I tried not to flinch as we passed the fountain. At the same time, I didn't look inside the basin, either. "Have you ever met the little girl?"

"Jack's daughter, Charlotte?" he asked, his voice warming. "Sure. She's a peach."

"She seems to have taken a shine to me. At least, she keeps appearing," I said, glancing back at the fountain and at the window where I'd first spotted her. "Before I can say anything to her, she disappears."

He led me under an archway choked with vines. "She used to like to watch me weed the daisy patch by the gazebo. It was her dolls' favorite place to play."

"I just wish I could talk to her. Even once. Can you help?"

He gave me a sideways glance. "She doesn't speak." He shook his head. "Poor little thing's been mute her whole life."

"Really?" I dodged an oak tree that had taken root in the middle of the path. "I never would have imagined."

"Don't be offended if she don't look you in the eye, either. She has trouble with that. But she's happy, or at least she was. I don't see her much anymore." He frowned. "That governess has got her locked up in the house."

I swallowed down my surprise and a bit of trepidation. I'd rather not go head-to-head with the governess again. But if I couldn't speak to the girl, how could I begin to understand what she was trying to communicate? "I suppose the governess has reason to be protective," I ventured.

"Would have been nice if they cared more when the girl was alive." He glared at the house. "Nobody gave a whit for her then. They thought she was slow. So what if she was? She was a sweet child and she loved my garden and my gazebo," he said. "Look at it."

A rusty iron bower rose up from beyond a tangled row of half-dead box hedges. Tobias passed through while I stepped over and around, the sharp, stiff branches scraping my legs.

He sighed, as if he'd come home. "This was her favorite place to play," he said, leading me to a spot less than twenty feet from the edge of the cliff. The gazebo leaned haphazardly on its stone foundation, flakes of white paint clinging in the grooves of the vine and leaf pattern.

"Our daisy patch was right over here," he said, leading me to a plot of mud and debris between the gazebo and the cliff edge. "I'd take extra time with those flowers and just talk about the plants and what I was doing." He swiped at the corner of his eyes. "She'd listen and play. I think we both enjoyed the company."

I stood near the cliff's edge and tried to imagine the lonely little girl playing with her dolls, unable to truly communicate, and found myself glad for the gardener who cared for her.

"Is this where she fell?" I asked, venturing toward the cliff face.

Just beyond the daisy patch, the ground grew rocky and uneven.

He lowered his eyes to the ground. "She ran straight off the edge. No one knows why."

I braved a few steps closer until I could see over the edge, down the sheer cliff face to the rocks and the road below. "Were you there?"

He floated several feet to my right. "Not when it happened. Her mother had asked me to cut her some fresh blooms from the rose garden, so I left her playing by the gazebo."

"Did Mrs. Treadwell request roses often?" I asked, wondering if it was a common occurrence or if something more sinister was afoot. The ghost of Mrs. Treadwell seemed to be the most tortured of the lot.

"She liked her flowers," he said.

"So no one saw Charlotte fall," I mused.

He hesitated. "They say not." He turned away from the edge, as if he didn't want to imagine it. He closed his eyes briefly. "Robert had gone looking for her. He was the one who found her, poor thing. He seemed to think her death had something to do with a curse they brought back from Egypt. Kept going on about it."

Perhaps he'd been right to worry.

Tobias glanced out toward the gazebo. "He said he needed to see Charlotte immediately, which was strange. He'd never paid attention to the child before. He said she'd touched something she shouldn't." Tobias drifted along the scrubby brush near the edge of the cliff. "That poor child," he mused, wandering away. "We must fix her daisies."

A chill settled over me from behind. I turned and saw no one.

"Tobias?" I called as I felt a sharp shove between my shoulder blades.

CHAPTER 14

I STUMBLED FORWARD, ARMS FLAILING, FINDING only air. *This must have been how she felt.*

Rocks jutted from below. I dropped to my knees on the hard ground at the edge of the cliff. Dirt and rocks tumbled over, and I could be next.

A harsh wind whipped past me, down the cliff face, tangling my hair in my eyes. My fingers dug into scrubby grass that came up in my hands.

Shaking, I back-crawled one inch at a time while I watched a small avalanche of ground fall headlong into the abyss.

I glanced back and saw the little girl, Charlotte, standing by the gazebo.

She stood, arms at her sides, serenely watching as I nearly fell to my death.

I edged back as quickly as I dared from the soft soil at the precipice, focusing only on the ground in front of me and the distance I was putting between myself and the drop-off. I made it several feet before attempting to stand, my knees weak and my legs unsteady.

I turned to face the little girl, but she had disappeared.

"Verity!" Lee emerged from the tangle of gardens between his house and the gazebo. He ran toward me, shock etched across his face. "I saw." The loose bottom of his gray work shirt flapped out behind him. He tried to catch his breath, his cheeks red.

"Are you all right?"

That was up for debate. "Did you see who pushed me?"

His eyes grew wider. "There was no one." He swallowed. "No one that I could see, anyway."

The shove had been hard and vicious.

"Charlotte was here." I hadn't seen her push me, but who else could have done it? Tobias, the gardener, had been too far away. He'd deemed her to be a sweet child, but that didn't mean she wasn't a vengeful ghost.

Or had the governess been angry at my exploration of the former arbor?

I scanned the area for Tobias. He'd certainly disappeared in a hurry.

"I'm so sorry, Verity," Lee said. "I never should have brought you into this."

"There was no one behind me. No one alive, anyway." That was the truly frightening part. "First the professor. Now this. How can we fight back against something we can't see?" Even with Frankie's power, I couldn't protect myself. If anything, it made me more vulnerable.

If I'd been standing a few inches closer to that drop-off, we wouldn't even be here discussing it.

"It's too much," he said, shaking his head. "It's not worth your life. It wasn't worth the professor's." He ran a hand over his face. "We have to end this now. I'm so sorry I even called you."

"Lee," I began. It was bad. I knew that. "I didn't mean we should quit." That wouldn't solve anything. "I get that this is freaking you out. Believe me, I'm in that boat too." I was the flipping captain. "But if we don't stop this, more people are going to die at Rock Fall."

I refused to be responsible for that. This ended. Now. With us.

"Fine. Then I'll lock it up, barricade the road," Lee said, going sixty miles an hour in the wrong direction.

Like that would stop the curious. As soon as Ovis wrote about the artifacts—and he would—Lee would be inundated. "We're too far into this to stop."

He kept going. "If this is about vegetables, I can give you more. If it's about your reputation as a ghost hunter—"

It went far beyond that. "You called me because I have experience with this and let me tell you plain: it's extremely dangerous to get the ghosts riled up and then leave. If we were going to do that, you're right, we should have never started at all. But it's done now and we need to see it through." Besides, he wasn't the one going in there. I was. "I've handled plenty of tough situations before." Although nothing like this.

From Lee's expression, I could tell he had his doubts.

"We don't have a choice," I said. "I need to go into the house anyway. I have Charlotte's doll." If I gave it back, maybe she'd stay away from me. I didn't like seeing her near the cliff. Or in my car.

He gave me a long look. Grudgingly, he dug in his pocket and handed me the key. "I hope I don't regret this."

So did I.

I still had to visit the little girl's bedroom.

He sighed. "If something happens to you, I'll never forgive myself."

"I'm being as safe as I can," I assured him. "Believe it or not, that was me being safe on the cliff back there." I'd maintained a distance from the edge, or I would have gone over with that powerful shove. I knew how to be smart about this. It gave me a fighting chance.

"You can return the doll," he said, glancing at the copse of trees that hid the house. "After that, I'm not making any promises."

A cell phone rang and it took me a second to realize it was mine. It sounded from the bag I'd left on the ground back by the cliff.

Lee seemed a bit startled. "That's a police siren."

"It's my ringtone for Ellis Wydell," I said, fetching the bag and the phone.

Ellis had used his police cruiser to pull me over more than once. I figured it fit.

Lee eyed the cliff while I answered.

"I thought you'd want to know," Ellis said, "they're calling Dale's death a heart attack."

"You don't sound like you believe that." I didn't either. It was too convenient that he'd visited the cursed house and then suddenly succumbed despite his otherwise good health. I was sure Rock Fall had something to do with it.

"I want to take a closer look at the study where he died," Ellis told me. "Care to join me?"

"I'm standing in the gardens with Lee right now," I said, eyeing my reluctant employer. "I'm going in with Ellis," I said to Lee, who didn't appear at all relieved that he'd have two people inside the house instead of one.

"Get in and get out," Lee said. "This doesn't change how I feel."

Yes, well, maybe finding that canopic jar would.

As he walked me to the front of the house, I saw no more sign of Tobias or the little girl.

I was running out of chances, and time.

Ellis arrived soon after, slamming the driver's side door of the police cruiser before making his way to my side. He wore a dark gray sheriff's department T-shirt, but I could tell from his jeans that he was off duty.

"What happened?" he asked, seeing the way Lee and I stood together. The man could read body language like nobody's business.

"I'll let her tell you," Lee said before directing his next comment to me. "Be careful."

Ellis shot me a questioning glance as the older man returned to his garden, and on the way up to the house I told him about Lee's doubts. I didn't have a chance to talk to him about the cliff. Truthfully, I didn't want to relive it so soon after. Besides, we'd already made it to the door of the mansion, and rehashing my fears would only complicate what we had to do.

I slipped the key into the lock. "If Lee decides to end this and close the house for good, this may be my last opportunity to fix things."

He nodded. "Show me the study."

Sunlight streamed through the windows of the mansion, but the atmosphere inside felt tense, as if a gun had been cocked.

The parlor stood formal and empty, with no sign of the weeping mother. Ellis tensed when I led him into the Egyptian room. The statues lining the wall appeared to watch us as we passed. I put that out of my mind and focused on the shadows they cast over the wooden game tables.

Yet I couldn't help but glance to the far right corner of the ceiling, at the irises cut into the ornate plaster molding.

"What's up there?" Ellis asked.

"Nothing." I saw no sign of the jagged shadow from before. "This is Jack Treadwell's study," I added, bringing Ellis to the threshold.

He stood for a moment at the entrance, observing. "This is where you found the jars."

"Three of them, as well as Jack's journals."

He stepped into the room. "Show me what Dale Grassino was doing when he died."

I edged past him toward the stack of books I'd seen the professor hand to Lee moments before we left the room. "These are all the books we've found so far. We were bringing Professor Grassino to see them when he came across the jars."

Ellis nodded, observant, careful not to disturb anything. It was a far cry from how we'd conducted ourselves in this room before.

"We were looking for the fourth jar, the one with Imseti on it," I said. "It would be about twelve inches high, and the face of a woman would be painted on the lid."

Ellis stood over the professor's death spot. I could still see the wisps of white light as they spun toward the heavens.

"He died holding the jar with the head of a falcon on the lid," Ellis said. "Investigators found it under his body."

"The falcon is Qebehsenuef," I said.

Ellis glanced at me. "What does that mean to you?"

"Nothing sinister." At least not that I could recall. "Qebehsenuef represents the west. The jar contains the remains of the intestines. He's protected by Serqet, who represents animals, medicine, all good things."

Professor Grassino had taught me well. He'd cared about me and about all of his students. He was a good man.

Ellis stepped over a pile of papers toward me, shaking me out of my thoughts. "What about Imseti?" he pressed.

"Imseti represents the south and is protected by Isis, goddess of nature and magic."

Ellis thought for a moment. "Does Imseti contain the heart?"

I saw where he was going, with Jack dying of a supposed heart attack. "Imseti contains the liver. The heart stays with the body."

"Which you saw in the music room, but is now gone," he finished.

"I could probably still see it," I told him. "It's on the ghostly plane. Where it is on the mortal plane is another matter."

Ellis nodded. "Police searched the kitchen, the dining room, every room in the house. They found empty crates in the attic, but no artifacts besides the three jars."

Dang. "So there's no basement."

"The rock makes it impossible."

"I see the police took Qebehsenuef with them," I said, noting the falcon-headed icon missing from the collection.

Ellis stood over the desk. "So if we have a killer—living or dead—and they're not after artifacts, what do they want?"

"I have no idea," I said, moving to the journals. "Maybe the professor discovered something in one of these," I said, picking up the one marked April 1910.

"Did the professor show a special interest in any journal in particular?" Ellis asked.

"We looked at the later volumes, but he didn't have much time to read them before he…" I didn't want to say it.

Ellis scanned the desk. "Perhaps he set a book apart from the rest." His gaze fell on the whiskey bottle. "There's no dust on that bottle."

"Lee and the professor were handling it," I said. The glass next to it appeared clean as well. "It's old scotch," I said, reaching for the glass.

"Don't." Ellis blocked me just as I caught myself.

"Wait," I gasped. "I saw Jack's ghost drink it. It might have gone bad since then. It's more than a hundred years old."

"MacKinlay's is only going to get better with age," Ellis said, crouching in front of the bottle. "But if Jack drank it and died, and now Dale might have drunk it and died..." He glanced up at me. "There are poisons that mimic the symptoms of a heart attack."

"Oh, wow." I took a closer look and I could see the traces of a drink at the bottom of the glass, and it wasn't one-hundred-year-old dried, either. There was no dust on top of that film of scotch.

"Detective Marshall should have seen this," Ellis said grimly. I didn't comment. Pete Marshall had never been my favorite person in town, nor I his. "I'm going to bag it," Ellis said.

He had supplies in the car. I joined him while he collected the evidence and waited with him while Duranja drove out from the station to pick it up.

"You okay?" Ellis asked as the other officer left down the path.

"I think so." It would be good to know what happened at least. But if my professor had been killed by a hundred-year-old murder plot, then the question remained: who killed Jack? "If Jack wasn't killed by a curse, that means an actual person had to have done it. But that person would have to be dead by now," I reasoned. "Perhaps we're not dealing with a curse but a vengeful spirit. Maybe that's who tried to shove me off the cliff earlier."

Ellis's mouth slacked. "When were you going to tell me that?"

"Believe me, I wasn't looking forward to it." The shove near the gazebo had scared me out of my wits. "All the spirits here have problems, but do you think one of them was a murderer in life? That ghost could still be here."

"Let's not jump to conclusions," he said. "We'll stick to the facts. That said, until we find whatever ghost or—" he paused

"—whatever *force* tried to kill you, Lee is right. This place isn't safe for visitors, or us."

I couldn't believe it. "So we're just supposed to lock up and leave when the answers could be waiting inside the house?"

"Dale is dead. Someone tried to kill you. We can't stay here." He held out a hand. "Give me the key. I'll lock up for you."

"I'll do it," I said, brushing past him. I'd have to come back later, without Ellis or Lee. "While you're here, I'll show you the cliff, the burned-out arbor, and the carriage house." Maybe Ellis would see something I'd missed.

Inside the house, I heard weeping.

I stiffened. "It's the mother."

"Is she saying something?" Ellis asked, opening the door.

"No. She's just crying." I stepped inside. "It's coming from one of the upper floors." Not from the parlor, as before. Her voice floated down the main staircase, sad and forlorn.

Ellis joined me at the bottom of the stairs and we exchanged a glance. I was about to suggest we check it out when the front door slammed closed behind us.

CHAPTER 15

"WHAT THE—" ELLIS STRODE TO the door and tried to open it. "Look outside. See who closed it."

I had a feeling it wasn't anybody he'd be able to see.

I peered out the window in the parlor, and just as I'd suspected, no one stood on the front porch or on the lawn. "I can't see anyone, dead or alive."

Ellis inspected the hardware. "It's locked," he said, letting go of the knob, not bothering to mask the surprise in his voice.

"All right." I tried to ignore the hair rising on my arms as I returned to the front door and inserted the key. It slid into the lock easily, and for a second, I thought we were okay. But it wouldn't budge when I tried to turn it. The handle didn't turn, either. "This is not ideal," I concluded, in the understatement of the year.

"Let me try," he said, taking my place at the door.

I let him have it. "There has to be another way out."

Grim faced, Ellis continued the struggle with the lock. "There's one door at the back, barred shut. Duranja called the fire marshal when he was in here yesterday."

"Well, then." I began to feel a bit claustrophobic. "I suppose a window will do in an emergency."

Ellis kept working while I tried to figure out how to pry open a parlor window that appeared painted shut.

We both jumped when a door slammed closed upstairs.

"Did you hear that?" I hissed, rubbing my aching fingers.

He had. Ellis's hand went to the small of his back, where he kept his gun. "Stay here. I'll check it out."

He went for the stairs, leaving his gun holstered for the moment.

"Wait." It wasn't like he could use a firearm against a spirit. "Let me go first."

I'd come here in order to make contact with these ghosts. They could be trying to tell us something.

I placed a hand on the bannister knob, straight into a spider-web. I stifled a screech and snatched my hand back, rubbing it on my dress as I rushed up the two steps to Ellis.

He moved slowly, cautious, which was A-okay with me.

There was something up there, and it knew we were coming to see it.

I removed the doll from my bag, her chipped porcelain visage staring up at me with dead eyes, her blonde hair tangling around my wrist. "We'll return this at the same time."

"All in a day's work," Ellis murmured, taking in every detail of our surroundings.

Torn strips of yellowed wallpaper cast strange shadows. Spider-webs clung to the occasional framed photograph of an unsmiling ancestor. Others had long disappeared from the wall, leaving only faint outlines and nail holes.

Ellis and I ascended the stairs side by side, and I fought the urge to take his hand. We had to remain alert.

"This place creeps me out," he said, lifting his hand to avoid a fat black spider scurrying down the bannister.

"Bet you're wishing we were back at your house, picking out curtains," I murmured.

The corner of his mouth lifted. "You're right. At least here I don't have to decorate." He glanced down the stairs behind us. "You know, I still have both curtains hanging—the moss and the light green one."

"Sage," I said automatically, stumbling when my toe caught a rip in the carpet.

He caught me. "It looks nice," he said, letting go. "My windows are covered."

"Men," I murmured, ascending the final steps and reaching the second-floor landing.

We paused, listening.

"I'm going to return the doll," I said. I'd place it exactly where I'd first encountered it, in the little girl's room.

I broke right, with Ellis directly behind me. Her door stood ajar, and when I pushed it all the way open, Ellis choked.

The back wall stood crowded with doll shelves, as before. Only this time, each doll had its head turned to look at us.

"Jesus Christ," he muttered under his breath. "Do it and let's get out of here."

My thoughts exactly. I pasted on a smile and walked slowly into the room. "Hi, Charlotte. I thought you might like this back."

I placed the battered, smiling doll on the bed and fanned out her hair on the pillow, like she was dead or something.

That might have been a mistake.

"Okay," I said, trying to be breezy, refusing to glance at the wall of dolls staring at me. "I'm always here if you'd like to talk."

Why did I say that? I shouldn't have said that.

I didn't want her at my house.

There was no sign of the ghost here. The room lay still as I backed away slowly.

Ellis touched my arm. "Let's go."

Gladly. I let out a sigh when we'd cleared the room, and Ellis gently closed the door behind us.

"It's okay," I said.

A large metal creak sounded from across the landing, like a faucet turning.

We froze at the sound of water spilling out hard.

"Oh, sweet Jesus," I exhaled.

"It's coming from over there," Ellis said under his breath, pointing toward the bedroom across the hall.

"I suppose we'd better check." I wasn't sure I wanted to see what waited inside.

Ellis nodded. The floorboards under the worn red carpeting creaked as we approached a white-painted door with a crystal handle. It did help, having him with me.

I was in the greatest danger here, even outside the house. As long as I was tuned into Frankie's power, spirits on the ghostly plane could interact with me, hurt me. At the same time, they were invisible, or sometimes merely shadows or scraps of movement, to everyone else.

"You ready?" Ellis asked, bracing himself. He twisted the handle and pushed in the door.

I half expected to see the little girl on the other side.

We entered a well-appointed woman's bedroom. Pale blue wallpaper fell in sheets from the walls. A cracked mirror with gilt trim struggled to remain upright against the onslaught.

A canopy bed in yellowed white silk stood with its back to the wall. Spiderwebs hung in an eerie cascade from the canopy to the stained coverings, forming a single tattered veil that fluttered with every exhale.

"Looks normal," I said. For a creepy, abandoned house.

It had to be better than what lay beyond this bedroom.

"You've been spending too much time at my place," Ellis quipped, studying every detail.

A carved marble fireplace lay cold in front of a pair of Queen Anne chairs. A haunting wind whistled down the flue, stirring the ash from a long-dead fire. Spiderwebs formed an intricate lace over the perfume bottles on a crowded dressing table. I wondered if the dried, flaking remains inside were indeed perfume or if they hid something more sinister.

If Jack had been poisoned, someone in the house had slipped it into his whiskey. He might not have been the only target.

A low thump sounded from the room just beyond, and with an eerie screech of pipes, the water stopped.

"At least we know where to go," Ellis said, low under his breath.

He stiffened next to me as the door creaked open.

From the next room, I heard the gentle sound of water lapping.

I forced myself to speak. "This way," I murmured, stepping forward to investigate.

Ellis merely nodded.

To the right, black mourning dresses still hung in the closet, *her* dresses. I detected the faint hint of rose perfume.

"I'm sorry to intrude," I said to the mistress of the house, hoping she had indeed invited me here. Someone had, with the running water and the slamming of the door, not to mention my inability to escape out the front. "You have a lovely room."

I pushed the bathroom door open, steadying myself against the eerie creak.

Cracked tiles shifted under our feet as we ventured inside.

Perhaps Annabelle Treadwell had gotten over her crying jag and wanted to talk. Maybe she'd seen what had happened to the professor. Or what had nearly happened to me.

A vintage sink on skinny iron legs stood directly ahead, bleeding rust onto the floor. The mirror above it reflected the focused, protective visage of Ellis, the man I'd been able to count on, no matter what.

"No water in the sink," he said, as if he'd expected that.

I had as well. The water had run too hard, too long. It would have overflowed a sink.

That still didn't prepare me for the moment when I turned the corner and saw the claw-foot tub filled to the brim.

"There it is." I stopped short. "You see the water?"

"Yeah," Ellis breathed out behind me.

It was filled with real water. A drop clung to the metal faucet and we watched it lose its grip and plunge into the tub.

What else did the ghost want us to see?

I drew closer and stood over the tub. Annabelle Treadwell lay dead at the bottom.

"Oh my God." I closed my eyes for a moment. "Oh, Ellis."

"What?" he pressed, staring down into the same water, searching.

"You can't see her." Of course he couldn't. This was for me, although I had no idea what to do about the poor, dead woman in her bath. She wore a black mourning dress, the ribbons at the collar swirling toward the surface. Her dark hair fanned around her head like a halo.

She almost looked as if she were sleeping.

I swallowed the lump in my throat, kept my voice steady. "Annabelle?" I asked gently. "This is Verity. I'm here." She gave no reaction. "Tell me. What can I do to help you?"

Her eyes snapped open and I'd never seen such a look of terror.

"Annabelle!" I reached out to help her out of the water and then caught myself. There was nothing I could do to save her. Her suffering should have ended more than a century ago. I couldn't lift her. Even a touch would be painful for both of us.

But I couldn't just stand and watch her suffer.

Robert had tried to rescue her and he died right after. Still, I wasn't Robert and I couldn't just let this happen. It wouldn't feel good, but if it helped, if I had a chance to get her out of there...

I'd just touch the water...

Ellis grabbed my wrist. "Tell me what you're doing."

"She's trapped!" I exclaimed, shaking him off. Annabelle gurgled. She reached for me. Something was holding her down. She screamed in soundless horror.

My fingers broke the ice-cold surface.

A terrible chill gripped me from behind, shoving me face-first into the water.

CHAPTER 16

A HARD GRIP HELD MY HEAD from behind and shoved me down, through the icy water, toward the terrified Annabelle. The invasive, sick wetness of my attacker's touch shocked me to the core as the ghost pushed me down harder.

Annabelle disappeared into nothingness.

My nose slammed against the porcelain bottom of the tub, and pain radiated through my face. Desperate to breathe, I scrambled to get a grip on the edges of the tub, to force myself out.

Ellis yelled, his words garbled by the water.

I kicked and hit something solid. It gave me enough leverage to turn onto my back, but a strong blow had me down again. It pressed hard against my chest and arms, an invisible weight holding me underwater.

I gripped the sides and pushed with all my might. My lungs burned and I nearly panicked when I saw the ghost's powerful male forearms take shape over me, with no body attached.

One hand shoved my chest, the other held my shoulder, refusing to let go. Ellis clutched me at the shoulders as well, shouting, his fingers digging into my flesh as he strained to lift me up.

But the ghost was stronger.

Ellis couldn't strike my attacker. He couldn't see him. Couldn't feel him. He could only fight for me by trying to pull my body away from the force that held it down. Both of us were losing.

I opened my mouth and water poured in. *Frankie!* I screamed in my mind.

I needed Frankie to cut the power, to get me out of this place where a ghost could talk to me, touch me, kill me.

But I'd left Frankie at home.

Ellis gave a mighty yank and my upper body barely breached the surface. "I got you! I got you!" He lunged for me, water sloshing, using his body to try to block me from the ghost. I spit water and took in a desperate, greedy breath.

The ghost moved straight through him and closed a hand around my neck.

"What do you want?" I screamed at my attacker, trying to force him off.

"It's mine." The ghost's voice echoed off the tile, a man's voice. "Give. Up." He squeezed. I gasped. Bit by bit, he forced me under.

My muscles burned, my lungs seized as I fought with everything I had, even as the water lapped over my cheeks, my nose, my face.

I didn't do anything!

The ghost took on solid form as he fought us, revealing a soaked white dress shirt and broad shoulders. He had a sharp jaw, prominent chin, and killer's eyes. It was Robert. And I knew if I went under again, I was dead.

I gripped the ghost's forearm, the dank, invasive touch radiating through me. I wished I could reach his eyes, and grimaced as my nails dug in hard. At the same time, Ellis gave a mighty yank. My shoulders popped out of the water, and I scrambled for leverage.

Robert shoved a booted foot onto my chest and drove me under. Ellis lost his grip. Through the lapping water, I saw Ellis scrambling in terror and the ghost's triumphant smile.

No!

Only now the governess stood behind them both. She held aloft a silver candlestick.

Ellis, watch out!

With a vicious sneer, she cracked Robert on the back of the

head.

His grip slackened.

I pushed past him, up, up, out of the water. Ellis grabbed me and held on tight. Gulping air, I let him drag me out of the tub, right through both ghosts, eliciting a cry from the governess as we connected in a tangling of energies.

She dropped the candlestick and retreated, her back to the wall, trying to wipe away my touch.

"I've got you," he said, steadying me as he stood on my attacker's head. Robert was huge, at least six foot five and pure muscle. I heaved, the water pouring off me.

"Quickly," the governess said, recovering. "He will be angry when he wakes."

I was angry now. "He was her brother!" I managed, catching my breath, fighting off the shakes. "Did he kill her?" He must have. He just tried to kill me by drowning, the same way Annabelle died. "What does he want?"

"We don't know," she said tightly. "He holds this house captive." The right half of her mouth turned down in a scowl while the scarred left side remained eerily rigid. "You have to leave!"

I might not have listened to her the first time, but I sure did now. Ellis and I fled the bathroom, and the second floor altogether.

Our soaking shoes slipped over the moldering carpet, but that didn't slow us down a bit. We attacked the stairwell with me in the lead. My head felt light and I stumbled twice, grabbing the creaking, dusty bannister for dear life, sending up a cloud of dirt as we nearly fell over ourselves getting to the front door.

I twisted the handle, but it didn't budge. "No!" I struggled against it. "You win! We're leaving! What else do you want?"

To kill us.

"Give it to me." Ellis battled the door while I tried the windows again. They were not only painted shut, but I didn't even see any latches.

I grabbed an iron bust from its pedestal and hurled it at the window glass. It bounced off and smacked against the floor. "Let us out!"

A dark mist began to form over Robert's death spot.

"Ellis!" He couldn't see it. I had to warn him.

The governess stood halfway down the stairs, a picture of calm. Probably because she was already dead.

The mist darkened and formed jagged edges. I'd seen this shadow before.

She held the candlestick aloft like a beacon. "He's coming."

Oh my gosh. It had been Robert all along. "Now, Ellis. We have to go now!"

He shoved away from the door. "Let's try the back."

"That door is barred," I huffed, chasing him through the hallway off the music room, past the dining room table set for dinner.

If we got out of here now, I was never coming back. Never, ever, ever.

"This is our only shot," Ellis said, stumbling through a dark butler's pantry crowded with wood crates. We burst out into a kitchen that looked like it belonged in the 1920s, with a cast-iron stove, an icebox, and a long wooden prep table at the center. He rushed past a large metal coal bin to a back door that had an honest-to-goodness iron bar padlocked over it.

"Shoot it!" I told him.

"That only works in the movies." He cursed under his breath and rattled the lock. "I need to bash it with something," he said, backing away, searching for a tool.

"Here's a teapot," I said, grabbing a rusted kettle and watching the handle come off in my hand.

I tossed the pot. There had to be another way out. Only we'd need a ladder to reach the high, broad windows—if we could even break them open.

The sky had gone gray. The sun was starting to set.

A low, throaty chuckle echoed from the front of the house.

"He's coming," I warned. Dang it. I sounded like the governess.

"I can't get it open," Ellis snapped.

He wanted to protect me. It was in his DNA. But I was easy pickings for the spirits and there was nothing Ellis could do about it.

Then I saw something that made my head spin and my throat go dry. There, at the foot of the narrow servants' staircase, hovered a thick white candle on a single candlestick.

Why did I ever think I could do this for a living?

"Ellis..." I started.

The candlestick was of this world, but not the soul who held it.

He turned and saw it. "Oh, my God."

The heavy antique candlestick floated in midair. And from one breath to the next, a flame flickered to life on the wick.

"Get behind me," Ellis said, abandoning the door.

"It could be the governess. She used a candlestick like that to bash Robert's head."

"And the time before that, she attacked you on the stairs." He drew close, placing himself between the hovering candle and me.

I appreciated the thought, but whatever wanted me was going to go straight through Ellis.

We watched as the candlestick began to float up the servants' stairs.

We had to move. Now.

Ellis touched my arm, as if he needed to make sure we were both sane, alive, and solid. "It's getting cold," he said.

He was right. Goose bumps skittered up my arms and I glanced to the butler's pantry. The same dark mist I'd seen at the front door snaked across the floor, blocking our only other exit. "Let's take the stairs," I said, rushing for them.

"Are you crazy?" Ellis whispered, joining me, keeping one eye on the hallway to the front of the house. Robert would be here any second. "Do you trust her?"

The candle paused halfway up the narrow staircase, as if it waited for us.

No. She hadn't exactly been friendly the first time we'd met. But she hadn't tried to kill us either.

"I choose to trust her," I said out loud, grabbing Ellis's hand.

The stairs were steep and dark, with no rail. I braced a hand against the wall for balance and kept going—up, up—deeper into the house.

"This could be a trick," he said in my ear.

"It could," I answered, out of breath, out of options.

It was better than facing Robert.

As we fled, he was regaining his strength downstairs. We had to escape him...somehow.

Breathlessly, we followed our mysterious guide up one flight of stairs then another, until the door at the very top creaked open and the ghost of the governess shimmered into view.

Her harsh black dress blended into the darkness behind her, as did her slicked black hair. It gave her the appearance of a scarred, disembodied head floating above the candle. Her good eye glittered, the bad one obscured by a corded mass of scar tissue. "There is one safe place," she hissed.

We'd take it. "Show us."

She turned quickly and led us out into the third-floor hallway. Darkness was falling fast. The candle shone through the ghost as she led us past the abandoned playroom.

"I don't like this," Ellis muttered.

"I hear you." But we didn't have a choice. And I had a feeling I knew where she was taking us—to the one place in the house that she controlled.

She stopped outside her private room, the one with the plain brass bed and the sad little hope chest, and she showed no emotion at all as the door creaked open.

"Wait. Why are you helping us?" I asked.

Her eyes hardened and her nose flared. "Take shelter or you will die like the rest."

"Come on," I said, urging Ellis into the pitch-black room on the third floor of a locked haunted house.

He joined me. He trusted me, even as his grip on my hand tightened. "This doesn't feel right," he said, a second before the door slammed closed behind us and a key turned in the lock.

CHAPTER 17

"WE'VE CHANGED OUR MINDS. WE need to go now!" I called, pounding on the door. But the ghost of the governess—if she was still out there—didn't respond.

Seemed she had us exactly where she wanted us.

I reached for Ellis in the dark. "I'm sorry...I—"

"It's okay," he said, wrapping his arms around me. "We'll figure it out."

I didn't see how.

We weren't only trapped in a haunted house, but now we were on the third floor with no way out, a questionable ghost helping us, and an angry ghost on the loose. My bag and Frankie's urn were back in the bathroom. Our cell phones were soaked from our struggle in the tub, and we still hadn't discovered any more than we knew before.

"Let's think this through," Ellis murmured, slipping away from me. I heard him move deeper into the room.

I followed, listening to his harsh, deep breaths. "Ellis?"

He clicked on a flashlight, casting a circle of light over the locked door.

"Where did you get that?" I asked.

"Back of my belt. Police-issue MagLite."

Thank goodness for small miracles. And cop boyfriends.

His light caught the narrow bed in the center of the room. A white coverlet crawled with gnarled vines, poised to reach out and snare the unsuspecting. I took a calculated step back. Not that I thought the coverlet was alive. It better not be. But in this house, you couldn't be too careful.

This room had freaked me out from the start, because it was clean—as if the governess were still alive and able to touch the world of the living.

The sticky sweet scent of decaying jasmines lingered in the air.

The beam caught the tilt of the roof over the front of the house and two windows that peered out like watchful eyes.

"We can open one of the windows and signal for help," I said, looking for a latch on the closest one. The upstairs windows were visible to everyone in the neighborhood below. Surely, if we were to lean outside, perhaps shine the light, someone would see us and help. The latch didn't budge. "Oh, come on."

Ellis tried the other one. "It's jammed."

More likely, it was being held closed. The governess didn't want us to leave. Robert, either.

Well, I wasn't going to cower in the dark, trapped by an angry spirit. "We'll break it," I said. "Give me your flashlight."

Ellis let out a small chuckle. "Hold up, Xena, warrior princess. I actually learned how to do this."

"How?" I asked. He raised the metal light and smashed the butt of it into the window. His whack at the glass looked exactly how I would do it. Minus a bunch of the strength.

"Police academy," he said, hitting it again, and again. The muscles in his arms flexed hard. "The glass should have broken by now," he said, breathing heavily, frustration creeping into his voice.

Yes, well, this wasn't a normal window in a normal house.

He looked at the window as if he couldn't quite believe it was still whole. He hit it again until he was spent. And still, the window held.

"Okay, we'll think of something else," I said, refusing to lose hope. I moved to the shadowy washstand that stood between the windows and picked up the heavy earthen pitcher, shivering at the coldness of the handle. "We've handled...interesting situations before."

"Get back, Verity," Ellis said, placing himself between me and the window. I turned and saw a jagged shadow of a fully formed human slink down the glass. It had no face, no real depth to it. It bunched as it attempted to push in under the windowsill.

"You see it?" I asked.

"No, but it's ice cold over here."

"Don't go near that window." I watched as the dark energy concentrated outside, where the window joined the sill, testing, reaching.

If it got in and we were trapped, I had absolutely no fricking clue how we could defend ourselves.

I braced, ready to fight, as if that would stop a cursed spirit.

"What's it doing?" Ellis pressed.

"Nothing, yet."

When the dark form didn't get in under the sill, it slunk over the glass itself, pushing and testing. I watched with bated breath, but it didn't make it inside.

I drew closer to Ellis. "Maybe the governess did us a favor. So far, we're safe here."

The wood sill crackled and the shadow disappeared.

I glanced up at him. "It's gone."

He nodded a few times, no doubt adjusting his sense of what was possible. "I'd like to be able to get out when we want. Maybe she has a spare key somewhere."

"Let's look."

"I'd also like to find something pointed we can try on that window," he added. "Once we're sure the dark shadow is gone. It's still a good idea to break the window and signal for help."

He turned to the hope chest at the foot of the bed. "Let's see what's in here."

The scent of jasmine grew stronger and the room took on a distinct chill. "I'm not sure she wants us in there." I wasn't thrilled about upsetting the ghost who'd kept us safe. Then again, if she thought it was wise to keep us up here until the danger passed, that could be decades. Centuries. I doubted ghosts worried about such trivial matters as food and water.

I held the light for Ellis while he unfastened the clasp.

Stiff hinges creaked in protest as Ellis lifted the lid. "Give me some more light," he murmured.

I shone it down and my beam was snared by an old wooden Ouija board.

"Don't touch it," I whispered. "Those things are bad news."

"I need to see what's under it," he said, lifting it out, setting it on the tangled vines of the bedspread. I swore I saw a tuft of dust spring up. Or perhaps it was something *in* the board. I didn't like this one bit.

The board appeared to be from the turn of the century. Bat wings sprouted from a sneering skull and embossed on either side of it were the words *yes* and *no*. Below, black letters and numbers stretched out in four rows, in old English style. At the bottom left and right, pentagrams stood vigil over the words *hello* and *goodbye*.

"It's a funny thing to keep in a hope chest," I murmured.

Ellis crouched in front of the trunk and reached inside again. "Look at this," he said, removing a triangular wooden pointer with a dull crystal set in the middle.

"That's the planchette. It's what the spirit uses to communicate. It moves it over the board."

Why couldn't the governess have kept something normal in there? Something useful? Like a glass cutter and a flare gun.

Ellis placed the planchette on the Ouija board, which was an exceedingly bad idea in my opinion. But he was more focused on exploring the chest. He ran his hands along the bottom, apparently not caring at all about the threat of chatty ghosts, spiders, dead rats, or even rusty metal bits...

"Here's a tarot deck," he said, holding it out to me, his head bent over the chest.

"Put it on the floor." I wasn't touching anything that belonged to an occultist ghost.

I wondered if the Treadwells had known about their nanny's ties to the spirit world. Maybe that was why the governess was spared from whatever evil Jack had brought back from Egypt. She'd found a way to protect herself.

"Tablecloth," Ellis said, unfolding a square of deep purple velvet. He placed that on the floor, along with a small, dry foot with three toes and claws at the end.

"Is that a chicken foot?" I asked.

"Looks like it," Ellis said, placing it on the tablecloth. "Maybe it does the same thing as a lucky rabbit's foot."

I didn't see how it could.

He leaned back from the chest. "Anyhow, that's it."

Good. "Close it." That chest creeped me out. "Maybe there's something in the tall dresser."

"It's worth a shot," Ellis said, straightening, leaving the chest gaping open.

I tried to ignore it as I tucked the flashlight under my arm and started on the top drawer. It was filled with underthings, and I immediately felt like I'd invaded the ghost's personal space.

But she was dead. She'd never wear these things again. And maybe, just maybe, she kept a door key, or perhaps a small sledgehammer, under her unmentionables.

Or at least a very hard rock. I'd give anything for a silver jewelry box right now, one with a pointy end.

"Let's think about this," Ellis said, in a tone that made me cringe. Not because he was wrong, but because I didn't exactly want to examine our situation here. For goodness' sake, we had an Ouija board on the bed while I went through a ghost's underwear drawer.

"Let's assume your professor's death was an accident," Ellis said, while I exhaled firmly and began on the next drawer, this one filled with stockings. "Let's say he drank the whiskey in Jack's office and it was poisoned."

I stopped. "Do you really think—?"

"The simplest answer is usually the right one," he said grimly.

It made sense. That would have killed both Jack and my old professor. Darn Dale for whatever he was celebrating with that old whiskey.

I eased a tuft of silk stockings back into the drawer as best as I could. Ellis had sent the whiskey to the lab. "When will we know?"

"In a day or two."

If we lasted that long.

I heard him move toward the bed, his footsteps echoing on the hardwood. "Duranja's cousin is head of the main lab in Jackson."

"I love small towns." I shone the light behind him, onto the Ouija board. The planchette hadn't moved. Thank God.

The light also illuminated Ellis, who was leaning up against the foot of the bed. "Now if Dale was poisoned, his death was an accident. Dale wasn't attacked."

"That's good," I said. I supposed. Although it certainly didn't bring him back. I started in on the next drawer: one filled with meticulously folded blouses. I patted them down, trying not to disturb the creases. "I still don't understand why Robert attacked me in the tub." I hadn't done a thing to the ghost.

Except invade his space, ignore his warning, and try to talk to his dead sister. But I'd been doing that the day before as well.

"Are you sure it was Robert?" Ellis asked.

I turned to Ellis. "There's no doubt in my mind." I'd never forget Robert's cruel eyes and the hard slant of his mouth. "It could have easily been Robert on that cliff as well. I didn't see who tried to push me over, but I'm sure it was a ghost." No mortal would have had time to get away.

The light cast dark shadows across Ellis's features as he thought. "You were safe the first time you saw Robert and the first two times you came here," he reasoned. "What changed?"

"Nothing." I'd shown up with good intentions, ready to help each time.

"Something shifted," he concluded. "What did you see?" he pressed. "What did you say? Think hard."

"All right." I rubbed my hands on my arms, trying to warm them. "Lee and I entered the house with no problem. Except for the run-in with the governess." I'd told him all about it. "We brought my professor the second time. I met Robert. I saw the artifacts on the ghostly plane and encountered a jagged shadowy *thing* in the Egyptian game room, but the spirit didn't attack. Lee, the professor, and I looked through the journals. Professor Grassino died," I added, wishing I could change it. I owed it to him to figure this out. "This afternoon, I spent time in the garden, but I'd already been out there once before with Lee. Lee goes there all the time and he's fine." At least I hoped he was okay. "I saw where the grape arbor burned and found a candle holder there. The gardener basically admitted it belonged to the governess."

"Then you were attacked," Ellis said as I bent to open the last drawer. "There has to be something we're missing."

"The governess was the only survivor. She most likely set the fire, but she's not the one attacking us." At least I didn't think she was, not after she gave us shelter tonight. I scooted over as he crouched down to help me search. We found two side-by-side stacks of carefully folded skirts, with nothing around or under them. But I could tell Ellis's mind was on what could have happened to cause Robert to go after me. "I don't understand why he wants to hurt me," I insisted. "Ghosts like me."

He stopped and braced an elbow on his thigh. "You keep saying that, but I don't think it's true in this case."

I hated to think that he could be right.

"Hey," he said, taking my hand, helping me up. "We'll figure this out."

"I sure hope so." There was nothing of use in the dresser. Nowhere else to look for any hard objects. "I had such hopes for breaking out," I said.

As I spoke the words, a circle of fog formed on the window closest to us.

Ellis's fingers tightened on mine. "You see that?" he murmured.

"Yes," I said under my breath.

It was as if someone let out a hot breath on cold glass.

Slowly, we watched the condensation inch across the window until it formed a perfect circle.

Don't freak out.

"What do you want?" I asked, keeping my voice steady.

A tiny fingerprint appeared on the outside of the window.

Ellis cursed under his breath.

The little fingertip paused. Then it began to creep across the glass. With a child's unsteady hand, it drew a closed, mostly triangular...

"Coffin," Ellis murmured.

"Maybe it's a..." I tried to think of something more pleasant. But he was right. Little Charlotte—if I had to guess—had given us our very own casket.

Ellis strode over to the window and took hold of the shade.

"That's not going to discourage her," I warned. She'd practically joined me in the tub the other day.

"I know," he said, gently lowering it, and the shade on the other window as well. "I just don't want to look at that. Not after tonight."

I understood completely.

"Come. Sit on the bed with me," he said warmly.

I shone a light on the narrow mattress with the Ouija board resting at the bottom. "Not on your life." I could stand all night if I had to.

He sat and I heard the crackling of the rope mattress frame. "It's not so bad." He leaned his back against the wooden headboard, opening up an arm for me to snuggle under.

I was being invited to snuggle with my ex-fiancé's brother on a ghost's bed while trapped inside a haunted house. Was this my life now? "If a year ago, you'd told me..."

He gave a wry smile. "Don't go there."

"Fine," I said, "only for you." I forced myself to join him on the tangle of embroidered vines. The mattress sank in the middle, which made it very easy for me to slide down next to him.

I shone the light toward the ceiling and tried to forget where we were. The heat of him felt so good and I sighed out loud when he wrapped an arm around me.

"I suppose we're staying over," I said. Ironic, since I hadn't allowed myself the pleasure since the night I'd spent at Ellis's place when he'd been injured. We weren't even dating then.

He kissed me on top of the head. "I have to admit I've been wanting to spend the night with you," he said. "Although this wasn't the way I'd pictured it," he added with a touch of irony.

We'd taken our relationship slow since we'd been outed by a ghost. It had been my choice and his. Now that we were an official couple, we wanted to take the time to really get to know each other, and I had to admit I was enjoying it. I leaned up and pressed my lips against his chin, his cheek, his forehead.

"Now you're just teasing," he said, finding my lips.

His mouth slanted over mine, and I leaned closer, feeling the heat of his body and the strength of him beside me.

We deepened the kiss and he groaned as we pressed tight against each other. Oh, yes. I could definitely get used to this.

I broke away. "We'd better stay alert."

"Right," he said, his lips brushing my cheek.

We lay in the dark together, and despite the dangers we'd faced, I found myself enjoying the warmth of him and the way he held me. Ellis had a way of making me feel *safe*. With him, I was part of something bigger than myself.

I snuggled tighter. "Thanks for being here with me."

He kissed the top of my head. "I wouldn't want to be any-where else," he vowed. And I knew it was true.

I closed my eyes and, quite by mistake, fell asleep in his arms.

The next morning, I was awakened by a shake from Ellis. "Verity," he whispered, "wake up. The door just creaked open."

"What?" It was barely light. I struggled to see.

"It's only open an inch," he said, helping me up. "I stayed awake. I saw. Come on."

My eyes adjusted and I could see it. The door stood open. Barely. "Robert can probably get in now."

"And we can get out," he said, taking my hand.

"Right." I'd somehow lost my shoes in the night. "Wait," I said, reaching for my sandals where they lay next to the Ouija board at the bottom of the bed.

We should have put that thing away. Although I wasn't going to touch it.

I slipped one sandal on, then dropped the other as the planchette on the board stirred.

"Look," Ellis said, pointing at the bed.

I rushed to join him at the door, one shoe in hand. "Let's go."

He hesitated in the doorway. "I want to see what it says."

Him and his investigative curiosity. "It's not supposed to say anything. It's supposed to wait until we play the game," which would never happen.

The planchette rattled against the board before inching over the X, the Y, the Z, until its pointer rested on a single word: *Goodbye.*

We ran. Down the hall, down a flight of stairs to the second floor landing. We made a quick pit stop into the bathroom on the second floor to grab Frankie's urn and my bag. Then we hit the front stairs like the house was on fire. I'd pry the door off the hinges with my fingernails if I had to.

Ellis reached the foyer first and swung open the front door like it had never been locked.

"How?" I stammered.

"Who cares?" he declared, seeing me out and then slamming the door behind us both.

CHAPTER 18

H E DROVE US BOTH TO my place. I wasn't in any shape to pilot the land yacht.

"That door just…opened," I said as we rattled down the hill in his police cruiser. "Why did it open for us this morning?"

"I don't know," Ellis ground out, keeping his grip on the wheel and his eyes on the road, "but we're not going back."

"We're not." I planted my back firmly against the seat. That was the last straw. I'd had enough. To heck with ghost hunting and curses and murderous spirits. I'd get a part-time job at the cleaners, and at the library, and perhaps at the gas station, and maybe the coffee shop. Nobody at The Frothy Coffee would try to kill me. I'd cobble together a living and never have to worry about seeing ghosts again because I wasn't even setting foot in the town funhouse next Halloween.

We pulled up to my place and found Suds standing in the driveway.

He took his bowler hat off and waved it when he saw us. I had Ellis cut the engine before we drove straight through him.

The ghost frowned at me, but I found it hard to care. Ellis had been right. Not all ghosts liked me, and right now, I didn't like them so much either.

Ellis killed the engine. "I'll walk you to the door."

"That's okay," I said, giving him a kiss goodbye. "Suds is outside. I'm going to see what he wants and then head in."

"All right," he said, drawing me close. "I'll call you this afternoon to check up."

We shared one last kiss before I let Ellis go.

"It's about time," Suds said before I even had a chance to open the car door all the way.

"I've been busy," I said to him. I turned to wave as Ellis drove away.

"You screwed up big," Suds barked. "Frankie's almost spent."

Frankie.

I couldn't imagine what this adventure had done to him. He'd never lent me his power for so long. "Where is he?"

The poor ghost had lost his feet, his legs, his torso and his arms on regular ghost hunts, ones where we'd turned the power off after several hours. His bits and pieces always came back when he rested, but I'd never pushed him so hard before.

"This way," Suds said, his manner stern. "I was just about ready to visit you in that god-awful place and make you come back."

"I wish you would have," I said, rounding the house. Maybe Suds could have gotten us out of there.

Or he could have gotten hurt.

Frankie sat under the apple tree in the backyard. At least, from the position of his disembodied head, I assumed he lounged. On second thought, it appeared as if he leaned rather awkwardly.

"Oh, Frankie," I said, rushing to see what I could do.

Part of his chin had gone missing and his cheekbones caved at a worrying angle. His forehead was entirely see-through and it appeared as if his face were ready to collapse. "I'm so sorry," I said, crouching next to him.

"So am I," he said, his cheek plastered against the hard bark of the tree, as if he needed it to keep him from sliding down.

"Don't worry," I said, fighting the urge to smooth the sweaty hair off his forehead, wishing I could ease his pain. I'd never seen him so disheveled. "I quit. I'm never doing this again."

"You *what?*" He flopped his head back onto the tree and glared up at me.

"I'm going to go inside and call Lee and tell him I'm not a ghost hunter anymore. We're done." Frankie would be off the hook. Lee would be glad to have everyone safe, and now I was as well. It just wasn't worth it.

The gangster worked his jaw. "Let me get this straight," he ground out. "You drained me...for *nothing*?"

I glanced back to Suds, who stood behind me. "Can you give us a second?"

Suds rolled his eyes.

"Listen, doll," Frankie spat, trying to straighten his head, which lolled alarmingly to the side. He was going to tip over at this rate. "I once drove a shipment of pistols and hooch from Cleveland to San Francisco on a half tank of gas and a prayer. And did I quit? No!"

He wasn't making any sense. "You couldn't possibly have done that," I said, due to the physics and the fact that I couldn't imagine the gangster praying over illegal gun and alcohol shipments. Then again, this was Frankie...

Frankie grew so angry he shimmered. "That's not the point!" he yelled, making me fall backward onto my butt. His lip curled in pleasure at my shock. "You are going to get out there and do your job. I didn't lose my entire body so you can quit before we get paid."

Of course it was about the cash. The jerk. "Some things are worth more than money," I told him, climbing to my feet.

"Name one!" he shouted.

Like I was going to debate him when he was in this mood. "You're not going to change my mind on this, so you might as well disconnect me and start gathering your energy back."

He slammed his head against the tree so hard that he disappeared straight into the trunk. Served him right.

I turned and almost walked straight into Suds. "Take care of him," I said, stepping around the ghost.

Suds shoved his hands in his pockets. "I always do," he said, gliding next to me. "Now when are you gonna start?"

That was rich. I turned to face him. "I let your entire gang take over my back porch *for Frankie*." Frankie's body would return in time if he took care of himself. I looked around at the empty backyard and porch, devoid of whiskey bottles, flappers, and gambling tables. "Where did everybody go?"

Suds stiffened. "The Eighteenth Infantry is hosting war games again. They like to reenact their battle and see what went wrong. Our guys play the other side because they like to shoot things."

Seemed they'd taken the party with them. But Suds had stuck around for Frankie.

It softened my annoyance. Somewhat. "He'll be okay," I assured the ghost.

An awful trumpet sound bleated from my back porch.

"Frankie?" I asked, seeing his disembodied head lying cheek-down next to my daisy pot. He gave the instrument another blast, making it doubly clear he had about as much musical talent as a dying giraffe.

"I still have lips. I'm going to play the trumpet!" he declared.

Suds and I exchanged a glance.

"All day!" Frankie added, bleating the trumpet again. "I'm not turning your power off, either," he said as we approached his concert porch. "If you don't want to ghost hunt, you can listen to my concert."

"How long until his lips give out?" I asked Suds when we'd reached the back steps. "Or until someone takes the trumpet away?"

"Fats McGee is passed out in the pond," Suds said, as if he wasn't quite sure what to do. "I have no idea when he'll wake up."

Well, it wasn't as if I was going to swim down to find him. "Frankie," I said, stopping over the prone head of my friend. Enough was enough.

He glared at me. "You going back to Rock Fall? Because Suds is going to play after me and he's not as good."

"Let me think about it," I told him, intending to do nothing of the sort. I mean, how long could Fats McGee sleep? Especially with that racket.

I went inside and greeted my skunk, to the tune of the worst trumpet blaring I'd ever heard.

I fixed a lovely blueberry and banana salad for Lucy and one for myself, to the out-of-tune bleats of "Reveille."

I could outlast the ghost.

Lucy and I read a book, or tried, as I realized Frankie's lungs were truly immortal.

I never imagined I'd grow to hate the sound of "Sweet Georgia Brown."

I threw open the back door. "That's it!" Frankie's head lolled on my porch, with a cocky grin too stubborn to fade. "You win. I'll go back!"

His grin widened. "I'll even go with you."

Joy. "Now stop it. Get some rest," I ordered. "It's going to be a focused, busy, absolutely terrifying day tomorrow."

And I had no idea what I was going to tell Ellis.

CHAPTER 19

THE NEXT MORNING, I ROCKED on my porch swing and tried not to think of the indecencies that might have occurred in that very spot over the past few nights. It was hard to think of much else with Frankie hovering to my left, just above a pot of geraniums.

He'd taken back his power after we'd come to our agreement last night, and I was glad to see he'd rested enough to regain his facial features and the loosened tie at his neck.

"Quit your lollygagging. Time to go." He lowered his chin. "You can't put it off forever, doll."

"I'm having breakfast. It's the most important meal of the day." I fished a blueberry out of my bowl and chewed slowly. "We should also wait until you've recovered more."

He huffed. "Nice try. We'll leave in five."

Hardly. "Ellis dropped me off here last night. I don't have a car." I selected another blueberry.

Frankie raised a brow. "Ellis and some other guy returned your car last night when you were asleep. It's parked out front."

"Dang." That was what I got for keeping an extra set of keys at my boyfriend's place. And for dating a considerate guy. "You don't understand," I said to the gangster. "Rock Fall is danger-ous. The house is haunted to the gills. I brought my old professor in to look at some journals, and now he's dead. At least one ghost is trying to kill me. A crazed, cursed archaeologist attacked me

yesterday when I came in from the garden." I sat up straighter.
"What if the garden has something to do with it? We should
walk the property again, maybe find Tobias." We could at least
go back to the burned-out arbor and talk to the gardener. We
wouldn't have to go in the mansion or be trapped anywhere.

"I like this. You're thinking." Frankie prodded, "Let's go."

I stood. "All right. Let me call Ellis." I'd ask him to join us,
preferably without dwelling too much on my dramatic change
of heart. I headed for the wall phone in the kitchen, depositing
my blueberry bowl next to the kitchen island for Lucy. She ran
for the sweet, juicy fruit, took one look at Frankie following me,
and made a mad retreat for the futon in the parlor.

"She can't even stand to be in the same room with my head?"
he balked.

"They say pets *know*," I mused, just to get his goat. Meanwhile,
I dialed Ellis at home. After a quick exchange of pleasantries, I
said it outright. "We have to go back to Rock Fall."

"Why? What happened?" he asked, on instant alert.

"Nothing awful." Yet. "I think I know why the ghost was
after me. I might have found something in the garden."

"Okay," he said, thinking. "I can't go today. I'm working. In
fact, I should have left already."

I wrapped the long phone cord around my arm, twisting it to
go with the churning in my gut. "The thing is, I can't wait."
It wasn't just the threat of Frankie going to town again on his
trumpet.

Last night, I'd been scared. I still was. But I didn't know what
to do about it. Now, I really wanted to retrace my steps to revisit
those gardens. There might have been something I missed. I
needed to know why the ghost was after me.

Besides, Charlotte had shown up at my house before. What
was to keep Robert from doing the same?

"I'll take Frankie," I said, unwrapping the phone cord from
my arm, stretching it as far as it would go. "And don't worry. If
something happens, I'll call the police."

"I am the police," Ellis said dryly.

"Right. I'll call you."

"With what? We soaked our phones last night."

"Dang." I'd forgotten. I hated to go in with no way to call for help.

I could almost hear him putting the solution together on the other end of the line. "Stop by the drugstore on the way out," he said. "I'd planned on taking you to dinner last night, but since that didn't work out, I'll treat you to a disposable phone today."

He always gave the best gifts. "That's even better than roses." At least for a girl like me.

"How did I end up here?" he wondered aloud.

I wound the cord around my finger. "You love it," I teased.

"You're lucky I do." The smile in his voice said it all.

"I'll be careful," I promised. Ellis liked to protect me, but it also meant a lot that he trusted me to be smart and take care of myself as well.

"I'm counting on it," he replied. "And, Verity, I spoke with Duranja this morning. The preliminary lab report showed no known poisons in that whiskey."

"That's good, right?" I hated to think of Professor Grassino dying that way.

"I don't know what to think. I ordered further testing. Just—" I could tell he was holding back "—watch yourself."

"I will," I promised before I let him go.

Sure enough, the land yacht waited out on my front drive. He'd even filled the gas tank.

"You'd better marry that one," Frankie said.

"Ha." If only I hadn't almost married his brother last summer.

I drove us to Jackson Pharmacy, and after a quick stop there, I activated my new disposable phone and slipped it into my bag.

It had been a remarkably simple transaction, except for the part where veteran cashier Velma Thrasher didn't understand why a young man like Ellis would have a purchase like that waiting for a sweet thing like myself.

Worry about what you can control.

Part of me couldn't believe I was actually going back to Rock Fall. And that Frankie was coming with me. I steered north down Main Street.

This time, it would work out. It had to.

"The attacks started after I was in the garden with Tobias," I told the gangster.

His head rested on my passenger seat, like it had been lopped off. "This make you squirm?" he asked, in a playful mood now that he'd gotten his way.

"Cute," I said, which made him frown.

His head rose off the seat back to its normal position, as if he had a body. "Don't get on me for being slaphappy. I'm just glad to be getting out of the house," he said, watching out the window as we entered the ritzy old neighborhood below the looming cliff.

"Yes, you've been alone and lonely these past few days," I mused.

He couldn't hold the act for long and broke out into a grin. "I won thirty g's."

"I need to take you to Vegas," I said, only half kidding.

He made a noncommittal sound. "Lost thirty-three."

Of course he did.

But Frankie wasn't done. "If a Bruiser McKinley comes knocking, you don't know where I am," he instructed.

"Maybe I don't want you lending me your power again," I told him, approaching the road to the mansion.

"You're stuck with it today," he said.

Moments later, I felt it begin to prickle along my skin and settle over me like a blanket of electric sparks. In a million years, I didn't think I'd ever get used to the feeling. "Thanks," I gritted out.

The ghost grew pensive as my ancient car dipped and struggled up the hill toward Rock Fall. This was it.

The mansion loomed silently as we passed, its windows eerily dark. Not that I looked too closely. I didn't want to see anyone looking back.

We drove around the rear of the property toward Lee's house and parked in his driveway. I didn't see his car or any sign of him.

"I hope he's all right," I said, seeing no sign of life inside.

I killed the engine and got out of the car.

"What? Is this a social call?" Frankie protested.

No. I simply wanted to begin this investigation as far from the main house as possible. This seemed to be a safe zone. Although now that I was here, I was worried about Lee.

"I'm going to go check on him," I said, making my way up the drive and toward the front porch.

Lee spent a lot of time in the garden, and if he'd seen something he shouldn't, he could be in real danger as well. I sighed. At least he wasn't tuned in to the ghostly plane like me. It would be harder for a ghost to hurt him.

But not impossible. Poor Professor Grassino hadn't even believed in ghosts until shortly before he died. And I doubted the spirits in that house had channeled the dead while they had been among the living.

Except, perhaps, for the governess. I wondered if her ties to the occult had spared her.

I knocked on the door. "Lee?"

"When was the last time you heard from him?" Frankie asked.

"I saw him yesterday." A lot had happened since then.

"Lee?" I knocked harder. Still, no one answered. I stepped off the porch. "Let's hope he's out."

I found it strange that he hadn't called to ask what had transpired with Ellis and me in the house yesterday, especially given how worried Lee had been about us going there in the first place. Something was definitely wrong.

"You ready to go?" Frankie's head prodded.

"I am." We'd continue our investigation and hope for the best. "If Lee comes back, he'll see that we're here." I stopped to gather Frankie's urn and my bag from the backseat.

"The faster we solve this, the faster we get paid," Frankie said, keeping his eye on the prize. I had to admit, if the gangster had one gift, it was tenacity.

"Just remember, you can't use the money to pay off Bruiser McKinley," I said, approaching Lee's lovely garden and the tangle of vegetation beyond. "He's going to want some cash he can spend on the ghostly plane."

"It's the principle of the thing," he concluded, drifting next to me. "I'm teaching you persistence, a valuable life skill. And once we have the dough, you can thank me by doing some updates to that ancestral home of yours."

He was calling me and my home old fashioned? "What sort of updating did you have in mind? You're from 1932."

"So's your light fixture on the back porch," he said, hesitating when we reached the edge of the cultivated garden.

It wasn't that old. From the 1970s, maybe. "I've been focusing on other things." Like paying for food and electricity. I didn't know how I was going to afford a new cell phone. We stopped in front of a low wall of overgrown rosebushes. "Are you sure you're up for this?" I asked.

He nodded his head. "I'm Frankie the German. Nothing scares me."

"Hold on to that thought," I told him.

Silently, we stepped into the wild section of the garden and I found the break cut into the thorny bushes. I turned sideways, sucking in a breath to avoid the inch-long thorns. Frankie passed straight through.

The remains of an ornamental garden lay ahead. Dead branches littered the rippling red brick path, and overgrown bushes spilled from their beds, their scraggly branches brushing my legs as we passed.

"I met the gardener who haunts these paths," I murmured, competing with the hum of insects. The hot morning sun mixed with humid air made me sweat. "His name is Tobias."

"Never heard of him." Frankie glided through a tree limb brought low by the weight of predatory vines.

"Maybe he doesn't get out much." We passed under the chipped and leaning trellis and into the tunnel beyond. I breathed in the stink of rotting leaves and kept my eyes open for...anything.

"I forgot how much I can't stand this place," Frankie muttered.

I hadn't. Dead ahead stood a small courtyard with a bubbling fountain. A stone nymph stood naked in a large round pool, her generous figure twisted in a coy pose as she held aloft a jug of water. I remembered this place. The last time we'd been here, the fountain had held doll heads.

I didn't see how it could get much worse.

We approached it slowly. Frankie let out a curse as water began to bubble from the nymph's eyes and streak down into the pool. "Move it! Move it!"

He disappeared while I did a fast walk past the fountain, refusing to even look into the basin.

When I'd cleared the courtyard, I blocked my face with my arms and broke into a run. Branches slapped my ankles and my elbows. It didn't slow me down a bit. "Frankie," I said, searching ahead for him. I rounded a corner and located my buddy near an overgrown boxwood. He stood with his back to a falling-down wall.

"That place..." he began.

"I know." A group of birds took flight, shaking the trees above. "Come on. I'll show you the grape arbor. It's right over there," I said, pointing to a bare stretch dead ahead on the right.

Frankie passed it right up. "Anything good in here?" he asked, moving to the carriage house beyond.

"Not exactly," I said, going to draw him back. The place appeared as abandoned and forlorn as it had the last time I'd seen it. "I met Tobias when I was peeking in the window," I said, noticing the shutter I'd broken. On the ground below it lay the stone cherub's head I'd used as a step stool.

Frankie flicked his eyes in every direction, as if he anticipated a surprise attack.

I hurried over to him. "You hear something?"

"Maybe," he muttered. "I don't like this place."

I stepped up onto the cherub's head. "I stood right here and looked at the cars inside." I peered through the rippled glass, with Frankie right next to me. Inside, we saw an open-roofed roadster and a turn-of-the-century truck. Both had rusted where they stood. Hay bales, blackened with age, littered the floor.

Frankie let out a low whistle. "Hotsy totsy."

"What do you see?" Because I was looking at a decaying mess.

Frankie scoffed. "You got a packed truck in there."

"Yes. Full of gardening supplies, most likely." It was the only thing they'd need in bulk out this way. Large bags marked *fertilizer* thrust from the back end. A tarp hid the rest.

"How much fertilizer do you need?" Frankie scoffed. "Looks to me like somebody was packing a score." He glided through the wall without me.

"For real?" I tried to see, but all I managed to do was press my nose up against the dirty glass. "I'm coming around." I hopped off the cherub and searched for a way inside.

I didn't have to try hard. The lock had rusted on the pair of arched wooden doors to my left. I bashed it with a rock and it broke right open.

Success!

For a split second, I debated the moral implications of being glad to have such an easy time breaking and entering, but that lasted about as long as it took me to toss the rock. Frankie and I had a ghostly mystery to solve.

I stepped into the musty garage.

"I was right," Frankie called from the truck. "They've got guns up front and crazy stuff in the back!"

"Let me see." I moved quickly to the truck, every step stirring up dust. I put a foot up on the runner and looked through the open driver's side window. Two shotguns rested on the front seat. "We've got to call the police."

"Not so fast." Frankie's head popped through the driver's side seat, scaring the bejesus out of me. "We've got a king's ransom in gold back here!"

"Gold?" I repeated, my mind racing to catch up.

"Those bags are full of gold doodads!" he exclaimed, losing

his hat, not even caring as it fell straight through the car and out
of sight. "You got three big statues of babes with no shirts. Let
me tell you: that is art. You got a mummy. You got gold beetles.
They look solid. Even if they're not, you got a necklace with
rubies."

"It's the find from the tomb," I said, scarcely believing it.

"Ain't that a kick." Frankie grinned. "If I knew a score like
this was coming, I'd have helped you sooner. Hell, I'd have broken in eighty years ago."

What a sweetheart. "Someone cleared these items out of the
house." Into what appeared to be a getaway vehicle that had
never made it off the property. "I don't get it," I said, dropping
down off the runner. "Who would kill Jack, Robert, Annabelle
and Charlotte, steal the treasure, and leave it here?"

"Who cares?" Frankie asked, his power surging. I felt it crackle
down my arms. "We've got the loot! We did it. We *finally* did it!"

We did. Lee would be so glad. If he was okay.

No, he had to be okay. He hadn't found the carriage house. He
didn't see. Heck, I didn't even realize what I'd seen.

"We're home free," I said, digging in my bag for the phone.
"I'm going to call Ellis. He and the police can secure this spot. I
don't want to touch those guns."

"Verity." His voice chilled.

"I don't care if you don't like the police," I said, spotting the
phone under Frankie's urn. "They'll help us. You'll see." I'd
look up Lee's number. We'd get him right over here. We'd fix
this once and for all.

"Not the coppers. Look," he urged. "It's creeping down the
wall."

"What?" I looked up and saw the jagged shadow. "Oh."

I didn't even have time to scream before it took the form of
a man, a large imposing man, before crystalizing into the full
apparition of Robert Treadwell.

This probably looked really, really bad to the ghost. I slammed
my back against the truck. "We're not stealing anything." Now
I understood why he hadn't wanted me or anybody else near the

house and its contents. This was his life's work. His and Jack's biggest discovery. And he thought we were trying to take it out from under him. "We only want to see what's here," I promised.

"It's mine!" he hissed, reaching for me.

"Run!" Frankie screamed, disappearing into thin air.

I used the split-second distraction to dash past Robert and out of the carriage house.

"Die!" he rumbled, chasing after me.

He had to realize that I didn't want his treasure. Well, maybe I did. For Lee. But what was a ghost going to do with it at this point?

And how was I supposed to outrun a ghost?

I tore through the ruined gardens, with Robert cold at my back. I didn't dare turn and risk a stumble. I leapt over gnarled roots and busted pavement and ran for everything I was worth.

I lost my bearings, dodged toward the mansion, and saw Robert appear dead ahead.

"Frankie!" I didn't know if he could fight the ghost in his condition, but I knew I had no shot.

But Frankie was nowhere to be found.

I turned and ran the other way, away from the mansion, away from the queen's treasure. I dashed past the haunted fountain, and a path opened up to my left, the one that led back to Lee's house. Just as I was about to take it, Robert shimmered into view several yards down the ruined walkway.

He sneered, gliding toward me.

I blew straight past, toward the gazebo and Charlotte's daisy patch.

The trees broke and I saw the cliff ahead of me. *Sweet Jesus.* I stopped dead in my tracks and a wall of energy slammed into the back of me, shoving me forward.

"What the—no!"

It surged ahead, carrying me faster than I could have run, straight toward the drop-off.

I fell to my knees and still it pushed me toward the precipice. I grasped at weeds. Clumps of grass and soil came up in my hands.

The energy at my back took my breath away and drove me forward. "Frankie!"

"I can't stop it!" he yelled, head hovering over the drop-off. "He's too strong!"

The ghost of Annabelle materialized in front of him, her eyes blazing and her mouth set in a rigid line. "Enough!" she snarled as I went over the edge.

Her energy slammed into me from the front, forcing me against Robert's strength from the back, trapping me like a bug between two pieces of glass.

I stared at the rage-filled mother in front of me before daring to look down past my dangling feet to the thin air and the sheer drop below.

CHAPTER 20

I FROZE. ONE WRONG MOVE BY me or either of the ghosts who held me and I'd plunge to my death. Annabelle gritted her teeth and shoved her power straight at me, through me. I felt it burn as it slammed against Robert's power behind me.

"You," she hissed, looking straight through me, her hate focused on the ghost at my back. "I see you now. You showed yourself yesterday in the bath when you tried to drown the mortal girl."

"She didn't belong in our house," he boomed.

"So you drown her. You push her off a cliff." Her eyes blazed with hate. "Just like you pushed my baby off a cliff."

Robert's power sputtered and his grip on me loosened. I slipped.

"That was a mistake. I was chasing her. It was a game," Robert entreated, from behind me. His power surged. "She fell! *She* did that!"

"You killed her!" Annabelle's eyes blazed and she let out a blast of power that pushed me against the wall made by Robert so hard it made my head spin. It squeezed my chest, making it difficult to breathe.

The shadows around Annabelle's eyes deepened. "I caught you looking in Charlotte's room after she died. What did you want?" She shoved again. The air whooshed from my lungs. "Tell me!" Annabelle screamed, pushing forward, thrusting Robert and me back. My foot caught the edge of the cliff and sent pebbles tumbling to the ground at least twenty stories below.

I could feel his hard, cold breath at my back. He tossed an arm out, hitting my shoulder, the cold wet impact slamming through me as he swept me away behind him. I landed with a thud on solid ground, shaking, thrilled to be alive.

I scurried away, keeping an eye on the ghosts.

Robert stood his ground on the cliff's edge, with Annabelle hovering over him. "Charlotte stole some property of mine," he said, biting off every word. "I would have found it and I would have been gone if you'd have stopped asking questions."

"Gone?" she gasped. "You would have just left? Left me to mourn Jack all alone?"

"I didn't have a choice," he shot back.

"You hurt me," she said, her voice eerily cold.

"What did you do, Robert?" Jack stood behind me and drew a pistol. Annabelle gasped when she saw her husband. He pointed the barrel straight at his brother-in-law.

I scrambled out of the line of fire.

Robert stared at Jack, tears welling in his eyes. "I didn't mean it. She was all I had left. She's my sister, for God's sake."

Jack leveled the gun at Robert's head. "What did you do?"

Annabelle glided to the side of her husband. "He drowned me." Her breath hitched. "I caught him in Charlotte's room after she died. I looked at him and I *knew* what he did. He chased me. He held me under water."

"You were going to tell everyone," he urged, eyes wild, backing away. "You didn't realize—*it was a mistake*. I just needed the jar with Imseti."

"My find? You killed my wife and daughter over a canopic jar?" Jack pressed, advancing on his former partner. "Did you kill me, too?"

The look on Robert's face said it all.

Annabelle let out a loud sob.

"You weren't happy," Robert said to Annabelle. He appeared flustered, unsure. "Jack was never around. I was doing you a favor. It would be you and me again. You would have liked that. Don't deny it."

"I said some things," she stuttered. "I was sad. I didn't mean them!"

"It was mine anyway. All of it. I located the dig site. I discovered the tomb! I went in first! I tried to catalogue as much as I could while he made a damned mess of the place. It was a disgrace. I did everything, saw everything, and he took the credit because he had the bank account. I freed you and myself!"

She gasped.

Robert sneered. "If you would have left things alone, you would have been a wealthy widow. I did it for both of us!"

"He was my husband!" she cried.

His expression went cold. "It doesn't matter. You're stuck with me. I'm never leaving until I get what's mine."

Jack pulled the trigger and shot him in the head.

The ghost of Robert crumpled to the ground.

Annabelle let out a wail and clutched her husband, who holstered the gun over his shoulder and embraced her. "I'm sorry," she said into his shoulder. "I'm so sorry."

He held her tight. "You didn't do anything wrong. You were upset and I didn't help you. I was confused. I was stuck. I'm not anymore." He smoothed her hair. "I didn't even know you were still here. All I saw was that jagged *thing* everywhere."

She sniffed into his shoulder. "Me too. I was so scared and alone. I lost you, I lost Charlotte. Robert hurt me so bad. The shadow followed me everywhere. I can't believe it was Robert," she sobbed. "He's so angry."

"He's gone now," Jack promised.

I hated to break it to him. "Robert is only stunned. A bullet can't kill a ghost."

I'd seen the way the gangsters shot each other for fun. No spirit death was permanent on the ghostly plane.

Jack's eyes widened, as if he'd never considered it. "Then what do you suggest, ghost hunter?"

I ignored how strange that sounded when he said it. "Let me

think." My mind raced. Robert had died here at Rock Fall, which meant he had immortal ties to the property just as the family did. And Robert seemed to have more power. He'd kept the family members from finding each other for more than a century.

But the ghosts themselves had done better against Robert than I had. The governess had stopped him, as had Annabelle, and now Jack. No doubt they'd be even stronger together. Perhaps it was my job to unite them and let them fight for themselves.

Jack and Annabelle might not even know that Charlotte still existed.

"Charlotte?" I called. "You can come out now." If she was even around.

I'd barely said the words when the little girl shimmered into view between the daisy garden and the gazebo.

"Do you see her?" I asked, pointing. "Your daughter is waiting for you by the gazebo."

"She's there?" Annabelle rushed for the falling-down structure, running straight through the ghost of her daughter. "Charlotte?" she called, searching. She was soon joined by Jack, but Charlotte didn't appear to notice either of her parents, nor could they see her.

She simply stared at me.

I gathered my courage and walked quietly toward the little girl, who could inspire more than one nightmare.

"Hello," I said when I'd gotten close enough.

She showed no recognition or emotion. She simply pointed toward the gazebo.

I glanced past her, toward her anxious parents.

"Is this where you liked to play?" I asked, crouching down to her level, hoping it was a good idea. "Tobias told me about your daisy patch. You are a big help."

Her nostrils flared and she stared at the ground. Again, she pointed to the gazebo, or rather, the base of it. It was made of loosely stacked white stone held together with gray mortar. Charlotte pointed to a grouping of stones where it appeared the mortar had worn away.

"Do you want me to play here with you?" I asked, removing a stone.

She nodded, her hair falling over her face.

I glanced back to her parents, who stood watching, their hands entwined.

"I met your mom and dad," I said, removing another stone. "They love you very much."

She showed no reaction. She merely stood over me. Hovering. Making me distinctly uncomfortable.

Tobias said she'd played here. Perhaps this was her special spot. If I had to guess, I'd say Robert had interrupted her game after he'd cleaned out most of Jack's office and realized he was missing the fourth canopic jar.

Oh, my God.

I worked faster, pulling away several more stones to reveal an opening about the size of my head. "Is this it?" I asked, reaching inside. "Is this what you want me to see?" The little girl nodded and my fingers closed over metal.

I slid an old iron doll bed out of the hole. It had been white at one time. Most of the paint had flaked away. Rust gripped the joints and stained a faded pink blanket. I caught my breath. "Oh, Charlotte. Is this your doll?"

She nodded and pointed to the ancient canopic jar with the human face that lay nestled under the tattered blanket.

I'd found Imseti—the missing jar—the doll that Charlotte had taken to her special spot.

Tears welled in her eyes and fell in fat drops over her cheeks.

"Sweetie," I said, wishing I could touch her, "it's okay. You didn't mean to take anything. You're a good girl. You showed me the doll."

She'd tried to tell me at the fountain by filling it with doll heads. She'd left a lovely doll outside on the porch for me to stumble over. She'd sat in the backseat of my car and showed me the doll. She'd even brought it to the edge of my tub.

She'd told me without words that she had the doll. I just hadn't understood.

"Thank you, Charlotte. I'll take good care of her," I promised. But that didn't help Charlotte. She was still so sad, so alone. I had to try to fix that.

She needed her parents. Each of the ghosts, it seemed, had been so wrapped up in their own world, they had been unable to see anything else. Robert hadn't kept them apart. A curse hadn't either. It was their own pain and the inability to see beyond it.

It had taken the confrontation in the tub for Annabelle to see Robert, and the showdown with Robert for Jack's eyes to be opened. I wondered what it would take for Charlotte.

I certainly didn't want to scare the child, but now that she'd shown me the truth behind the hidden jar, maybe she'd be open to me showing her something as well.

I resisted the urge to take her hand. "You've been such a good girl. I have a treat for you. Do you trust me?"

She nodded. I knew she did. She'd helped me, and now I was going to return the favor. "Let me help you find your mom and dad."

A tear rolled down her cheek and she nodded.

"Okay," I said, crouching in front of her. "We're going to play a game. It's called the Seeing Game." She blinked hard. "Try not to be afraid," I said. "I know that's difficult." I'd been scared out of my mind most of the time at this house. "Your uncle can't hurt you." I moved to the side. "See? He's not even mad any-more. He's sleeping."

She peeked past me toward her attacker, who lay prone in the grass.

"Now on the count of three," I continued, "you're going to turn around and the Seeing Game will let you see your parents. One."

Her lip trembled.

"You can do it," I told her, as if it were easy. As if I had any idea.

"Two." Out of the corner of my eye, I spotted Annabelle and Jack waiting behind her, their hands clutched together.

"Three!" I said as cheerfully as I could.

Charlotte spun around and let out a small cry. She ran for her parents.

Thank God.

Annabelle sobbed as she saw her daughter for the first time in a century. Jack scooped Charlotte up with a whoop and Annabelle closed her in with a tearful hug.

I sat back on my feet, knees on the ground, and marveled at that little girl's courage after all she'd been through. She'd kept her strength. She'd broken through. And she'd found her mom and dad.

I had the best job in the world.

After a moment, Charlotte dragged her father over to see me, pointing at me.

"I know," he said, chuckling, "she helped us, too."

She pointed more insistently at the canopic jar while Jack scooped her up in his arms again.

Annabelle fluttered her hands, as if she didn't quite know what to do with her reunited family. "Charlotte doesn't speak," she explained, watching father and daughter. "She never has. The doctors call it a brain condition."

"She's beautiful," I said. "And I understood her quite well once I stopped and paid attention."

Annabelle nodded. "There is a great contrast to be made between those who take the time to listen and those who don't."

"So true," I told her.

Still, I couldn't escape the idea that Charlotte had wanted to show me more a few moments ago. But we'd found the jar; we'd reunited the family. What more could there be?

I bent over the find, my back to the winds sweeping the cliff. With gentle care, I lowered the blanket away from the artifact and saw the jar had broken clear down the middle. Something glimmered inside.

Odd.

I gently separated the two halves, careful not to damage them, and revealed a ruby the size of my fist.

Oh, wow. "Take a look at this, Jack."

I wished Lee were here. Between this and the relics in the carriage house, he'd never have to worry about money again. He could preserve the house and its history for this generation and the next. I'd done it. And I found myself supremely grateful.

The ghost glided over, holding Charlotte. "Well, I'll be damned. It's the cursed stone."

I placed it on the ground. "Cursed?"

"Take it. Now. Or else he'll get it," Jack warned. "The queen used that stone to concentrate her power and gain her greatest desire, a land of her own to rule. In the wrong hands, it could cause disaster. When we didn't find it in the tomb, I figured it was just part of the legend."

But it wasn't. It was sitting on the ground in front of me.

I gathered up my courage. I'd already touched it once. I winced and picked it up again. It felt heavy and ice cold to the touch.

"He's coming back," Annabelle warned. Robert's body had disappeared, replaced by a dark mist. It began rolling toward us.

Jack lowered Charlotte to the ground and raised his gun, taking a shot at the swirling form. The bullet passed straight through and we heard the deep, sickening sound of Robert laughing.

"I won't let you shoot me again," he hissed. "Now give me the stone."

The governess appeared directly behind Jack. "Give it to him," she said coldly. "Now that he's found it, he won't stop until he has it."

"What's it to you?" I demanded. "Did he promise you something if you help him?"

"I'm protecting you. I'm protecting all of you. Now give it!" she commanded.

Jack turned to me, afraid. "Ghost hunter?" he asked, as if I knew what to do.

I didn't understand how Robert could touch the jewel or what he could do with it. But if he wanted it, that had to be bad.

Robert's spirit took form and swirled around Charlotte. "It's mine. I found it in Egypt. I hid it in the jar. Only I know how to use it. Give it to me or I'll kill Charlotte for good. I know how to do it."

He was powerful. I could see him taking the child.

The governess glared at Jack. "Do it now!" She raised her hands as Robert's energy swirled faster.

I nodded to the ghost. I couldn't save Charlotte from her uncle, but maybe the governess could.

"Fine," Jack hissed. "Take it. Give me Charlotte and leave!" Robert dove for the stone and Jack snatched up the child.

Robert let out a shout of victory as he touched the stone.

The blood red surface snapped and sizzled. Robert's presence grew jagged and darker. I glanced at a wide-eyed Jack, who shielded his daughter's face as we retreated from the powerful, angry ghost.

I watched in horror as Robert's spirit mingled with the stone, giving both the ghost and the rock an eerie glow. This could be really, really bad. This ghost was deadly enough without him gaining an ancient power, one I couldn't hope to understand.

Then Robert's spirit jolted. He let out a hollow, unearthly scream as the stone began to suck him down. I stepped back more, watching it pull him in, not willing to be anywhere close as the stone absorbed the murdering ghost's spirit. My attacker struggled and fought, just as I had when he'd tried to pin me under water. But it didn't change anything. The stone dragged him down until he was gone.

We watched as the last wisp of smoke disappeared into the stone.

"What was that?" I asked, heart pounding, throat dry. I wouldn't have been surprised to see the stone implode on the spot.

"The curse," Jack said, stroking Charlotte's hair, keeping his distance.

"I got that." But was it over?

No one else moved. So I did. I approached slowly, not about to touch the stone. I swore it pulsed with a heat and energy of its own. It seemed *alive* somehow.

And when I bent over it, I could see a shadow inside, barely. A dark, jagged presence.

The governess glided up on my left and I had to work not to flinch away.

"You ever see anything like it?" I asked, not really expecting an answer.

Her lips twisted into a rueful sneer. "His greatest wish in the end was to keep everyone away. And so he has gotten his one desire." Her dark stare bored into me. "That is the queen's curse."

She'd told Jack to offer the stone to Robert, to give the malicious ghost ownership. "Did you know it would capture him like that?"

"I hoped," she said coldly. "How else could we stop him?"

"True." I was sorry it had to come to that. "I never would have imagined such a thing existed."

She gazed down at me, serene with an edge of danger in her voice. "You'd be surprised what legends are true, ghost hunter."

I was always surprised in this line of work. "Is he trapped for good?"

"He is. Until he has a change of heart," she murmured. "I don't see that happening anytime soon."

"He cursed himself," Jack said, joining us. "He let his obsession with the stone take over his life, and ours. But not anymore. Never again." He held hands with Annabelle, who carried Charlotte. "He's gone for good."

And the rest of the family was free.

CHAPTER 21

OF COURSE FRANKIE SHOWED UP again, after it was all over.

"I knew you could handle it," he said, his disembodied head floating a safe distance away from the cursed stone. "I admit I'm not a natural ghost hunter. I prefer something I can shoot."

"That actually would have worked out in this case," I said, going to retrieve his urn. At least, it would have helped. I located my bag near the edge of the cliff where I'd dropped it. "I don't know what we would have done if Jack hadn't shot Robert when he did."

"You could have joined me on the other side," Frankie mused, as if it were no problem at all. "I could show you the ropes."

I glanced back at the cliff that almost ended my life. "You've got to be kidding. You're talking as if my death would merely mean a change of address."

"No," Frankie said, as if I was too daft to understand. "You wouldn't have to move at all. We could haunt your house together."

In his dreams. "I'd rather eat my own eyeballs."

He shrugged. "You're the one who trapped me. We have a bargain."

Joy.

He eyed me. "Speaking of our deal..."

I felt a prickling rush as his energy left me.

"Wait." I turned to see Jack and Annabelle playing with Charlotte on the lawn, before they disappeared. "I was going to say goodbye."

"We'll go back later, after they've had some time together," Frankie said. "They've earned it."

"Oh my." I smiled at my ghost friend. "Is that you growing a heart?"

He wrinkled his nose like he smelled something awful. "I certainly hope not."

Despite his faults, Frankie deserved a break after what he'd been through. He disappeared into the ether—where ghosts go to recover—while I called Ellis and asked him to meet me outside the carriage house.

Minutes later, my hunk of a deputy sheriff arrived with Lee and a half-dozen police officers.

"I stopped by to see you," Lee said. "You were gone, so I ran by to see Ellis and get the update."

"I can't let you out of my sight for a minute," Ellis said, folding me into a massive hug, not even caring about our audience.

That boy was sweet on me, and he didn't care who knew.

"Thanks again for the phone," I said, kissing him on the cheek, glad that he'd had faith in me to make this right.

I pulled away from Ellis and addressed Lee. "It's good to see you as well." I'd feared the worst when I couldn't find my first and only client today. "I was worried about you."

"Well, I was terrified for you," Lee said, shaking his head. "I'm so sorry I put you through this."

"I'm not," I told him. We'd stopped a murderous, vengeful ghost. We'd brought a family together. And…"You're never going to believe what Frankie and I found," I said, leading him through the carriage house door.

Lee cried when he saw his grandfather's greatest discovery

preserved for more than a century.

"It's too much," he said again and again as officers helped him open bags, trunks, and crates full of priceless artifacts.

"I need you to see something else as well," I said to Lee and Ellis. I led them to the ruby at the base of the old gazebo and told them the story.

Ellis, as usual, knew what to do. He removed the stone with a shovel and placed it in Qebehsenuef, the falcon-headed jar. With my vision strictly limited to the mortal realm, I no longer saw the shadows of Robert's spirit inside, but I knew he was there.

"It should be safe until we can store it properly," Ellis said. Even so, Ellis had insisted he be the one to carry the stone and the jar back to the carriage house. He turned and gave an order to Duranja. No one was to touch the artifacts.

"It's the best way," I agreed. The stone had been contained in a similar jar for the last hundred years.

Lee nodded. "It's my responsibility now. I'll make sure the cursed ruby won't be touched by anyone, not now—not ever."

"Your grandfather will be glad to hear it," I told him.

"So what are you going to do with it all?" Ellis asked. It appeared as if he had half the police force already guarding the find.

"I called that armored security company you recommended," Lee said. "They're going to keep it safe until I can call in some experts and learn what we have."

"What *you* have," I corrected.

He smiled. "I haven't forgotten about our deal. You get half, Verity. You've earned it."

"It's too much," I said, relief flooding me at the thought of receiving a tiny portion. I could buy furniture, fix up the house. I'd have room to breathe. I didn't need half of Lee's family legacy to do that. I'd let him calm down. Then, we'd talk.

"All I ask is that you tell me what the heck happened," Lee said.

"Come with me." No one else would believe it.

CHAPTER 22

THE THREE OF US SLIPPED outside and stood very close to the window I'd used to spy on the treasure before I even knew what it was.

"Robert killed Jack," I told them. "He admitted it to me. Although he didn't say how."

The two men exchanged a glance.

Ellis drew our group closer. "Did Robert say why he killed his brother-in-law?"

"He wanted Jack's find. And his life, from the sound of it. It seemed Robert was the one doing the work, at least according to him. Jack got the glory."

Ellis nodded. "So he killed Jack and they had a funeral instead of an unveiling of the queen's tomb." He stepped back. "Talk about twisted family politics," he mused. "At least nobody in my family resorts to murder."

I counted myself lucky for that.

"When Jack's family was in mourning, it made sense for Robert to disassemble the display in the music room," I said. "But instead of storing the queen's mummy and her artifacts in the attic, in their crates, he had them taken out to his truck." Disguised in fertilizer sacks.

No wonder the expedition boxes in the attic stood empty.

"Annabelle would have trusted him," Lee said. "He was her brother and her husband's business partner. I know my dad spoke highly of his uncle Robert."

If he'd only known. I looked out over the overgrown garden, at the ruin of it all. "The trouble started when Robert finished stealing almost everything and realized he was missing one of the four canopic jars."

"The one with the jewel inside," Lee said, glancing back at the carriage house and the find it contained.

Ellis frowned. "Either way, if he was going to go on another expedition and later claim the queen's untouched tomb was his, he'd need that jar."

Exactly. "It just up and disappeared on him. Charlotte had it. She loved dolls and saw a new one in her dad's office." She hadn't meant any harm. "Robert went after her. She ran. He says it was an accident. I'm not sure if he meant to harm her, but she went over the edge."

"That poor kid," Ellis murmured.

I hoped that Tobias wasn't listening, that he didn't feel too bad. When Robert had asked him if he'd seen the child, Tobias couldn't have imagined it would lead to Charlotte's death.

"Annabelle suspected, didn't she?" Ellis asked.

I nodded. "Jack Junior was due in the next day. She was upstairs and had begun running a bath when she caught Robert looking through Charlotte's room. She made some accusations; Robert grabbed her. She broke away and ran to her rooms and tried to hide. He drowned her in her tub."

"Maybe the tomb was cursed," Lee muttered, "to cause a man to do that."

"But how did Robert die?" I wondered. "He killed everyone but the governess, but she couldn't have known what he'd done, so it's unlikely she avenged the family. And it doesn't make sense that he'd just drop over dead."

"We'll have to ask her," Lee said, "that is, if you don't mind."

"I'd be pleased to visit the family again," I told him. Now that the ghosts were free and happy, his haunted house should be no problem.

"Yes, we need the whole story," Ovis said, stepping from

the overgrown bushes near the door of the carriage house. He snapped a quick picture of the inside before pointing his camera at us.

CHAPTER 23

WE LET OVIS HAVE HIS story. It was the least we could do. And, truly, there was no stopping him anyway. Half the town had already heard about the artifacts on the police scanner. Lee and I even posed for Ovis in front of Robert's truck. It was a heck of a find.

And when archaeologists went through it, they found an ancient vial with the remnants of agathodaemon, a very ancient, very lethal poison.

On further review, the long-forgotten toxin was found in the professor's body and in Jack's whiskey bottle.

Dale Grassino's death was officially ruled a case of accidental ingestion, but Ellis and I both knew the professor was an unintended victim of a century-old murder plot.

A short time later, Lee and I kept our promise to go back into the house. This time, we made sure we knocked before Lee opened the front door.

Jack sat in the parlor, smoking a cigar, while his wife did embroidery. Charlotte played dolls on the floor, with the governess looking on.

"Sorry if we're intruding," I said, fighting off a smile. "We just wanted to check in and see how you're doing."

Jack stood, his cigar in his mouth. He grabbed his whiskey off the table and came to greet us. "It's amazing," he said, clapping Lee on the back, his hand going straight through, "we're a family again." He stood close to his grandson. "And I'm so proud of you."

"I'll tell him," I assured the ghost.

Annabelle stood behind her husband, tears in her eyes. "It's a dream come true."

"I'm so glad you're happy here," I told them, and I was.

Charlotte inched between them, clutching a doll with a pink dress very similar in color to the sundress I wore. "I like your doll," I told her.

"Her name is Verity," Annabelle said.

Maybe I wouldn't think on that too much.

The governess stood near the stairs. "Can I have a moment?" I asked her.

She nodded and allowed me to walk her to the settee by the door.

"Thank you for saving my life," I said simply. "It was a brave thing to do, to stand up to Robert like that."

"I didn't want you here at first, but when you were kind to Charlotte…" Her eyes glassed over and she swallowed hard. "She never spoke to me in life, but after she died, she came through to me on the Ouiji. I stayed to protect her."

And it seemed she'd never left.

"I saw her hiding behind your skirts on that first day."

"She was afraid. So was I. No one had ever come into our house before."

It had been terrifying for all of us. "Did the darkness keep you in the house all those years?"

Her gaze darted to the floor. "When I was alive, I tried to free them. I could sense their spirits. I saw Robert's ghost in the arbor outside the carriage house. I went out at midnight to perform a ritual to try to untangle them from the dark presence. But when I lit the candles, the flames leapt at me. They burned me."

Robert hadn't wanted to go anywhere, not without his find.

"That was very brave of you to try," I told her.

She refused to meet my eyes. "I thought the Eye of Horus had protected me from harm. That my mystical talents had spared me when the family had perished." She let out a short laugh. "I wasn't special. I just wasn't a target."

"I'm so sorry you had to go through this alone," I told her.

"I had Charlotte." She turned her scarred side away from me and I let her have her privacy. She didn't want pity, just dignity.

"How did Robert die?" I asked.

She pursed her lips. "I don't know. Shock?" She swallowed and gazed up at the stairs. "When he came down that staircase, soaking wet, holding Mrs. Treadwell, I nearly fainted myself. Robert was mad with grief. I told him to sit down. That I'd fetch him a sherry."

I straightened. "Did you take it from one of the bottles on Mr. Treadwell's bar cart?"

She blinked, not understanding. "There was only one bottle there. I don't drink, so I can't say what it was. I'm sure it was as good as sherry. I doubt he'd have tasted it anyway. He wouldn't stop pacing. He only took a sip. Then he died."

So Robert had died of his own poison. I found it hard to feel sorry for him.

The ghost held my gaze. "I'm glad you stayed even after I tried to force you out. I feared for your safety and your life, but you were brave, and you set us free."

"Thank you for safeguarding us." Her room had been a literal lifesaver.

I doubted she'd have kept her job if the family had known their governess dabbled in the occult, but I was sure thankful for it.

"I did not die by Robert's hand. Just from old age," she stated simply, as if it were that easy to create the life she had for herself. "I protected myself and my space as best as I could."

"I'm lucky for it," I told her, "and for you."

A few weeks later, I hosted a dinner party at my house. Ellis brought the plates and the utensils. Melody supplied a chicken. Lee came bearing the most beautiful fruits and vegetables I'd seen yet. We'd invited the Treadwell ghosts as well, but they had each declined. Seems they were occupied enjoying their freedom and each other.

I served fresh asparagus and strawberry salad along with roast chicken and gravy.

"I'm so glad it all worked out," Melody said, having a second helping of strawberry salad. "Ghosts love my sister." She winked at me. "And so do I."

Most ghosts liked me, when they weren't in pain. Or playing poker out on the back porch. Frankie let out a whoop, which most likely meant he'd won another hand. That ghost was having a good night, and so was I.

After dinner, I snuck out onto the porch to check out his hand.

"Lucky at cards…" I said, watching him discard a two of clubs while keeping three kings and an ace.

"Unlucky at love," he answered, pulling a second ace from the pile. "I still can't believe you're eating at a card table," he said, adjusting the cards in his hand. "You could have made a mint off Lee Treadwell."

"Actually, it turns out I couldn't." Even if I had been greedy.

The complete set of canopic jars, along with the mummy and the effigies of the three princesses, proved Jack had found the tomb of the lost queen. Ovis's news article and photographs went global.

After almost a century, Jack Treadwell was finally famous. Well, in Internet terms, which meant it lasted less than a week.

Jack had missed the entire thing. He was too busy admiring his new afterlife.

As for Lee, the Egyptian government confiscated the artifacts. The queen's artifacts were a national treasure, and nobody should be denied their heritage.

Professor Grassino was praised for his role in uncovering the find, and the exhibit of the artifacts at the Museum of Egyptian Antiquities in Cairo would be named in his honor.

And the press did us some good. The Sugarland Historical Society committed people and money to make improvements to the house and set up a foundation to maintain it.

I did a few radio interviews around town, telling the story of my first ghost-hunting job and drumming up donations for Lee's cause.

"But what about you?" Frankie prodded, lowering his cards down to the table. "What do you get?"

"All the veggies I can eat," I told him. "Plus, Lee wrote a check for five hundred dollars out of his personal checking. He gave it to me tonight." He shouldn't have, but he did.

"It's not a lot," Frankie muttered.

"It's more than he can spare." Plus, it meant I could buy supplies for a little building project I'd been planning.

I motioned to my hunky guy to come on outside and he did, leaving the screen door flapping in his wake.

"You tell him?" he asked.

"Not yet." I wanted Frankie's full attention when I let him in on my plan to build his gang a shed out past the pond. The South Town boys would have a permanent place to get their rowdy on. Ellis even said he could add a raised area near the cornfield that could serve as a stage.

"Or you could not tell him and we can go shopping for a kitchen table," Ellis said. "I know someone who would give you a deal."

"The South Town boys need my help," I told him. "You get better bands when you have a stage."

Then maybe they'd pass out there instead of in my pond.

"I'll get a table after the next job," I told Ellis.

He wrapped an arm around me. "I know you will."

Frankie might not have been paying attention, but I had a feeling some of the other ghosts heard. The daisy pot rattled and I swore I heard a splash from the pond. Let them celebrate. Life on the other side should be good.

I was certainly grateful. We'd solved the haunting at Rock Fall. Ellis and I were together. And if I was lucky, I might—just might— be able to make a go of it as a ghost hunter.

The disposable phone in my pocket vibrated.

"I wonder who that could be," I said. I hadn't given out the number to anyone except for Melody and Ellis...and in that radio interview this afternoon. "Oh, Ellis. I think this could be it." I stepped away from him and answered.

The static on the other end of the line was deafening. A woman's voice crackled in the midst of it. "We need you." She sounded hollow, far away.

"Who is this?" I pulled the phone away to check the caller ID.

"I recognize that number," Ellis said. "It's the main number for the Sugarland Heritage Society."

I had a sudden, irrational thought that this had better not be his mother. Virginia Wydell had sat on the board of the society for as long as I'd been alive.

The phone crackled as I brought it to my ear again. "Sorry. I didn't catch your name. What can I do for you?"

There was no answer, and for a second, I thought I'd lost her. Then, the voice came through again. "There's been a murder."

New York Times and *USA Today* bestselling author Angie Fox writes sweet, fun, action-packed mysteries. Her characters are clever and fearless, but in real life, Angie is afraid of basements, bees, and going up stairs when it is dark behind her. Let's face it. Angie wouldn't last five minutes in one of her books.

Angie earned a journalism degree from the University of Missouri. During that time, she also skipped class for an entire week so she could read Anne Rice's vampire series straight through. Angie has always loved books and is shocked, honored and tickled pink that she now gets to write books for a living. Although, she did skip writing for a week this past fall so she could read Victoria Laurie's Abby Cooper psychic eye mysteries straight through.

Angie makes her home in St. Louis, Missouri with a football-addicted husband, two kids, and Moxie the dog.

Sign up at *www.angiefox.com* if you are interested in receiving an email from Angie Fox each time she releases a new book.

20682921R00125

Printed in Poland
by Amazon Fulfillment
Poland Sp. z o.o., Wrocław